MW00510120

THE DISHWASHER

Love is the one problem you'll never solve

EDDIE YOUNG

Disrupted Life Publishing

THE DISHWASHER

Copyright © 2020 by Eddie Young

All rights reserved. No part of this book may be reproduced in any man-
ner whatsoever without written permission except in the case of brief
quotations embodied in critical articles and reviews.

First Printing, 2021

for

MARY LATTIMORE

full of grace

CONTENTS

Preface

Finding a meaning to life is both a timeless and universal problem. The fortunate ones have taken comfort in the subjective solutions they have settled on and are understandably fearful of, or are even determinedly resistant of considering anything beyond that which has provided them with purpose and direction. Often in spite of the questionable validity of the signposts, some manage to push aside what corresponds with reality, and have grasped hold of scarecrows that point to an Emerald City.

But for us, the *unfortunate* ones, the security of an ordered universe that we lost along the way, isn't coming back. There is no comfort, no direction, and no balloons taking us back to Kansas. This problem brings nothing but despair, and that in and of itself is a problem. It is in fact a mystery that a solution should even be needed. But it is. And why some of us suffer through the absence of finding it, even to the extent of ending this hopelessness by suicide, alludes all understanding.

This book doesn't presume to solve these problems; no one can. It is, however, intended to illustrate the despair, and put flesh on the struggle. It's no fault of yours if you should be one who needs this picture drawn, our position is difficult to understand. So with that in mind, these pages paint a self-portrait of my own personal existential hauntings. Maybe you will relate, and find yourself not so alone in your affliction. Or maybe the following procession will feel strange and foreign to you, but as you watch those like me from the yellow brick road, and consider our dilemma, know that we didn't ask for this. Trust us, no one would ask for this.

This is not an autobiographical work. It is a fictional story based on my life and my thoughts on life. The arc is precise, and there are real events woven through. As for the characters, a few appear as themselves in real biographical settings, and others, while remaining true to themselves, have taken on fictional roles. Even as I write, I've learned that my friend Carol is dying from cancer, and it sends me into yet another state of paralyzing sadness.

To my shame, I don't know exactly how long she's been homeless; one day is too long. She was born against her will, and into a societal structure that she neither designed nor endorsed, and so lived, or was pushed, beyond the margins of it. It's foolish to think that we should all enter this world equipped to manage, much less flourish under structures that are arranged and dictated by others.

Carol never experienced the flourishing of life that she should have and is now investing her hopes in an afterlife. But then why wouldn't she? Who wants to believe that this is it? A series of random fortunes and misfortunes until your consciousness dissolves into the void. If there is an afterlife hosted by an omnipotent deity who's building mansions in glory, she deserves one.

Throughout my time spent in the homeless community, I've seen an overwhelming adherence to this trust, this hope swelling with expectation. Perhaps it's because this life here and now has so miserably failed them that they have no choice but to either give up or to embrace their misery as a mandatory prelude to paradise. But I've also witnessed this promise of heaven being used as bait by preachers and their churches who have no interest in this side of eternity, generally because their life predicament doesn't scream for it. They have more than what they need. And so their preaching, their songs of "This world is not my home, I'm justa passin' through," and their dramatic prayer services provide exactly what Marx described as an "opiate for the masses." And it's powerful. I've seen people live through the most excruciating despair and die unnecessary and undignified deaths, only to be reassured through my tears, that "at least they were right with god," or "that they're in a better place." And that says it all. Of course, they're in a better place, 'cause for many of us, anywhere is arguably better than this place.

However, let me be clear. Despite my contempt for the disgraceful spellbinding of the vulnerable, by those who have mastered and profited under these earthly systems, I have no desire nor intentions of suggesting that those who pursue and embrace a religious paradigm are on a fool's errand. No one knows what's real and what's not, especially the well-paid preacher who's been as equally spellbound by his paycheck. And providing that one's adherence to these religious beliefs brings peace, serves others, and harms no one, then I can think of no sound reason to judge them.

But for those of us who've dismissed religion and its narratives, there's still the sense of, and even an urge to acknowledge supernatural forces at work in our lives. Some for our good, and others for our destruction. And just because those in antiquity have organized these suspicions of the supernatural into seemingly strange and fanciful dogmas, doesn't mean that we should dismiss them as strange and fanciful. Why am I led to thoughts of suicide, when I would rather be happy and content with this life? Why do I feel dragged down paths that I didn't choose, nor do I want to travel? And conversely, why, when against all odds, does life work out for certain ones, as though every threat were disarmed, and every obstacle removed? Are we being watched and manipulated from beyond? And do we have any say in it?

These thoughts once led me to consider the probability that if life has no meaning, and if we're nothing more than pieces being moved around on a board by these outside forces, then in the end, nothing really matters. But that's not true, because I know that if nothing else matters, this one thing does, and it's how you treat others. That's why we feel guilt over wronging someone, because it matters. And in considering the whole, there are energies that we can know for certain, fires that we feel towards one another, that we can't help fanning and standing next to. And who'll deny that the best of these energies is love? And love is the one problem we'll never solve. It is a problem within the problem, for it needs no meaning, no reason, no objective agreement.

So if we are to conclude that things do matter, while maintaining that life has no meaning, and it's absurd to look for one, could what matters make life worth living? And if so, can love be the reason that is unsurpassed by all others? Can this energy burn so bright with such a meaning and purpose of its own, that understanding the universe and confronting whatever forces it may release upon us, becomes inconsequential? Can love be a reason in and of itself? As Pascal said, "The heart has its reasons, that reason knows nothing about." And love is not bound to nor does it correspond with our reason. It doesn't concern itself with what makes sense, it persists against all odds, and that's where we find Juliette and Romeo. But of course, love isn't contained solely within the romantic, and that's where we find friends giving their last dollar to each other, and mothers who sell all they have, including themselves, to feed their children.

I don't believe love gives meaning to our collective existence, but that it can fill each personal moment of existence with meaning. Until, of course, the one we love leaves. And then the aching pain of emptiness returns. When I watched my mother being carried out of a small church building in a box, I folded up and sobbed like a child at the sight of it. Where did she go? The one who thought the sun rose and set on me, and the one whom I loved and owed my life to was gone to who knows where, and the moments she had filled with meaning left with her. And that mattered, and it still does.

So here we are, faced with our own personal Masada, a tragic inclination to take our own lives and refuse these forces the pleasure of taking it from us. But I'm convinced that love can make our short time on this fortressed plateau worth living, even while we watch the ramps being built below.

There's no place like home, and love holds the power of the ruby slippers, a hope in somewhere beyond this place, a hope in seeing them again, and a hope that you are waiting for me. I haven't forgotten you.

I'm almost there.

CHAPTER 1

Pray For This Cup To Pass

She looked out the window and sighed, "Je suis presque là."

It's one o'clock in the morning, and he's sitting on the cold, wet floor of a parking garage just off Seventeenth Avenue. He's underground, and the sounds of nightlife are humming beyond the walls above him. The garage is small and dimly lit, with support pillars running down the center, making it difficult for some, and nearly impossible for others to move their car out of its space.

He watches as another one attempts to work its way out. Back and forth, the tires squealing on the smooth wet floor with every turn, and the passengers' boisterous conversation distracting the already challenged driver. To avoid storming the affair, expelling everyone and doing it himself, he closes his eyes, turns the bottle up, and pleads with the negligent powers from beyond to show some mercy and release his mind from this torment.

The fuse is short these days, and his impatience with everything and everyone escalates into a rage as instantly as turning a switch. He's convinced the demon is manipulating even these most ordinary events to provoke him, to lure him deeper into conflict with, and surrender to this force that has finally chased him into a corner. He clenches his eyes, lowers his chin into his chest, and waits.

They almost always get it wrong, like this one has, who's stopped to reassess and study the next move. Their headlights expose Jaime and his sleeping friends. The driver returns to their starting position to try again.

He needs to be invisible. This is the night, and he doesn't want to be rescued by some pedestrian savior. "But then again, who really cares?" he asks himself. "I'm just another drunk holed up in a garage." Most people who frequent this area know it's a hangout for the homeless. He won't attract any more attention than a curious glance or a disgusted glare.

With his back pressed against the wall, and his arms resting on his knees, Jaime loosely holds a bottle of vodka in his left hand and his box cutter in his right. With a simple exchange of hands, the escape becomes permanent. His head hangs still, and he stares into the floor. As he begins to pass out, Ezra's voice registers, "Stay awake! You need to finish this."

Jaime turns to see Ezra's face reflecting in the pool of urine Bombay's lying in, and then looks away. "Give me some time," he whispers, with a guarded voice, as if to say, "Keep it down, others will hear you." He was never fully convinced that the others didn't hear Ezra. But they were only hearing what they believed was Jaime talking to himself. Except Bombay.

Unlike the others, he knew these one-sided conversations weren't just an endearing quirk, they're the anguished disputes with something or someone from beyond the veil. These moments would usually spill out at night while sitting around the campfire. Jaime would catch himself and embarrassingly look around at the faces in the circle to see who had noticed. Those who had would be discreetly laughing it off, but not Bombay. He would always be looking directly at Jaime with grave but sympathetic eyes.

The driver finally solves the problem and pulls out, restoring the darkness to Jaime's corner.

Drunk and struggling to focus, he lifts his head and looks around to see if anyone else has come in out of the rain. Carol and Rookie are crumpled up in the opposite corner, and Bombay lies in a fetal position next to him, all in a mercifully unconscious state. Dito's somewhere, but not here. Probably for the best. Monday and Briena must have decided to sleep in the woods, and Shelly was picked up by the cops a few hours ago for begging. "At least she'll be dry tonight," he thinks to himself. He looks around at the others who are scattered across the floor and takes a deep breath. The garage reeks of ripe humans and alcohol.

Streetlights break up the night along the avenue that runs adjacent to and just below the ceiling of the garage. Through the ventilation openings above his head, he can hear people laughing as they run from the rain after leaving the restaurants and bars that surround him. All of them are as oblivious to him as his sleeping friends. Their laughter takes over his thoughts and fills him with anger and resentment.

He remembers what it was like to laugh, to really laugh. But lately, laughter seemed to be nothing more than the release of bitterness, a surrender to the predictable despair he felt in nearly every aspect of his life. It's a self-generating descent into darkness. Despair breeds hopelessness, and hopelessness feeds the despair. Hearing laughter cuts what's left of your heart, and it all bleeds out in contempt and scorn. "How can they be so blind?" He wonders.

He lowers his head and stares back into the floor. The image of her lifeless body floods his mind. "If only they had seen her lying abandoned and disgraced under that bridge. If only they had held the beautiful and trusting hand of the one that life so casually betrayed, would they still be laughing?"

"Why are you laughing!" Jaime shouted.

"Sleep it off, you lousy drunk!" Someone shouted back.

"You don't even know!" Jaime yelled back at them.

"They don't even know," he said in a quiet, self-assuring voice, hurling his empty bottle across the garage.

Bombay raised his head and looked over his shoulder. "Are you alright my friend? Is he coming for you tonight?"

"Who?"

"The dishwasher, is he coming for you tonight?"

Jaime looked over towards the garage entrance, and there he was again. Ezra drifted by in the rain, turning to look at Jaime before melting into the large dumpster outside the corner of the building.

"I don't know, Bombay, I don't know. Go back to sleep. It'll be alright."

"Don't let him deceive you tonight my friend; pray for this cup to pass." Bombay turned over and drifted back into unconsciousness.

Jaime shouted at the entrance, "Leave me alone! I'm gonna finish it. I can do it myself. Just leave me alone!" He shuffled his feet and watched as the trash surfaced from a pool of water that had gathered at the foot of a drainage pipe, reminding him that even if he could change his mind, what was surfacing from that river would eventually pronounce his death sentence, and he'd rather not give another person that pleasure. "I can do it myself," he repeated under his breath.

"Are you alright, sir?" asked a young couple walking to their car.

Jaime tried to chase their eyes off of him while hiding the razor under his shirt. "Don't look at me! You don't know."

They shook their heads and walked away.

Jaime took his glasses off and rubbed away the tears that were welling in his eyes. "You don't even know," he repeated to himself.

The rain was beginning to fall harder now, flooding the gutters, and streaming through the cracks along the walls. With the campsite broken up, the scattered knew where to bed down to avoid getting soaked on nights like this, but there was no way of staying dry. Like the determined demons, rain finds its way in. As he watched the taillights of the last car leaving the garage, a clap of thunder startled him back into the moment.

Jaime set the box cutter on the floor between his legs, managed to light a cigarette, and reached into the pocket of his jacket for the other bottle, but it was gone. Remembering that he'd given it to Bombay earlier in the night, he crawled over and found it sitting on his pack, half empty. He didn't need any more to drink, as much as he needed the comfort that came from holding it. And Ezra was right, it was time to finish this, no passing out.

"Is that you, Jaimz?"

Still on his hands and knees, retrieving the bottle, his heart sunk when he heard Dito's voice. He turned and saw her unmistakable silhouette walking towards him.

"What the hell are you doing out here?" she asked. "Why aren't you in your bed? You don't do things good," she said with a laugh.

Jaime closed his eyes and breathed out a short laugh in return. You really couldn't even call it a laugh, he was scared, but Dito had a way.

"We do not..."

"Shut up Jaime," Dito said, still laughing. "I went by your place to get out of the rain, but you weren't there. Look, one of the volunteers gave me this umbrella when I told her I was banned from the mission," she said with a shrug of her shoulders. "I looked for you, what happened?"

"Sorry Dito, I just couldn't get in the mood to hear the preacher talking about how god loves me, but that I'll be standing in judgment for being a drunk."

Dito laughed again. "Yeah... what the hell's wrong with this goddamn umbrella!" She gave up trying to close it and threw it across the garage. "I'm sorry Jaime, I shouldn't have laughed. Needing to drink's not funny." She looked down at him with empathy and tried to lighten the moment. "Hey, they had barbecue! I brought some back in case I found you. Are you hungry? Probably not, you're never hungry."

"I'm alright, Dito. You can save it for breakfast."

"How come you're only wet from your boots up to your thighs? You been wading through... wait, what's that?" she asked, slowly pulling back her hood.

Jaime hadn't had time to put the razor away, so he clumsily tried to cover it with his leg. She looked at it, and then at him. Dito slid her backpack off and sat down beside him. He looked straight ahead as she gently locked her eyes on his. She knew he was stalling. He knew she was waiting.

"What's going on, Jaimz?" she asked, as she nudged her shoulder against his, trying to break his stare. "Here, let me have that, you don't need any more tonight," she said, as she gently pried the bottle from his hand.

"Don't pour it out."

"I'm not gonna pour it out silly, we're just gonna set it over here for a while."

She reached over as he turned his face away, and ran her hand across his cheek. "That's not rain, Jaime. What's wrong? You wanna talk about it?"

"Not really."

"Here, just let me have that, too," she said, reaching under his leg for the box cutter. "You don't gotta talk if you don't want to, but I'm gonna keep these things with me tonight, and you can also give me some of that cigarette," she said, nudging his shoulder again, trying to get that half-smile out of him.

She took a long drink from his vodka. "This is mine now, you're drunk, Jaimz." Looking around, she asked, "You don't have anything with you. No blanket, nothing. It's cold. What were you gonna do tonight?" They both went silent. He looked over at the garage entrance, but Ezra wasn't there. She followed his eyes and then looked back at him and then the razor. "What were you gonna do, Jaime?" she asked again in a sad, softer voice, as she realized he wasn't planning on needing a blanket.

She pulled his head over onto her shoulder. "You don't gotta talk about it. It's okay."

Jaime lifted his head and clasped his hands around the back of his neck.

"I'm sorry, Jaime. I know life's hard for you, but this razor won't make things right. I won't try and stop you, but I'll miss you."

Jaime released his hands from around the back of his neck and drew them forward along his jawline. He nodded. He would miss her, too. "But you're going south anyway."

Dito sensed the tension, looked down between her feet, and wanted to ease it, but she couldn't. Not knowing what else to say, she crushed the cigarette out on the wall. "Hey, don't worry about that now. It's late and I'm really tired. You wanna share my blanket?"

"I think I'll sit up for a while, Dito."

She downed the last of the bottle, showed it to him, and asked, "You don't got anything else hidden around here that I need to know about, do you?"

"No, nothing else hidden."

"You tellin' me the truth, Jaime?"

He tried looking away, but she reached over and took his glasses off, folded them, and slid them into his shirt pocket.

"You're tellin' me the truth, right, Jaimz?" She tried to chase his eyes down with hers, but he wouldn't look at her. He just nodded his head. "I hope so," she said.

He rubbed the tears from his eyes.

"Jaime."

He turned.

"Let's go to sleep. It's late, and you look like you've been crying for a thousand years. I'll hold you if you want."

"Mary..." Jaime said.

Dito slid down onto the floor, rolled her blanket out, and wrapped herself up, using her backpack as a pillow. "What about Mary? Is she in her new place?"

Jaime hesitated. "Yeah."

"That's nice." Dito stretched and yawned. "When you're ready, just come on over, this blanket's big enough for the both of us."

He lit another cigarette and waited for her to fall asleep, which never took long for those with a clean conscience, like Dito. She was curled up in the opposite direction of Bombay, both of them on either side with their backs to him. Jaime reached around and felt for the razor Dito was holding with both hands against her chest. He carefully pulled it away and tucked the blanket in and around her shoulders, stirring her half-awake for a moment. "Goodnight Jaime," she said, falling back asleep before she heard his answer.

He took the cross from around his neck and placed it around hers.

"Goodbye, Dito."

CHAPTER 2

It's all Meaningless

Jaime was hired to run the kitchen, and it was here, in this small restaurant, that he met the dishwasher. Ezra was a medium built man in his thirties. He had a stubbled beard, square jaw, pale blue eyes, and dirty blonde hair that he kept under his 'go to hell' hat- a worn European style cap that topped off his prominent forehead as though he'd been born with it. The only child of wealthy parents, who had thrown their disappointment out and into the streets before his twentieth birthday, Ezra spoke with a measured rhythm and the ragged voice of one who'd endured more than his share. His nerves were so stressed from the years of excessive drug use that he couldn't contain his shakes, which became more prominent when he spoke. His thoughts were hidden behind an expressionless face, until that insidious grin crept out, as it did upon seeing Jaime walking towards his station that first day.

"So, you're the new guy," Ezra said, without looking up from the plate he was rinsing. Jaime was being painfully forced out of his introversion and into a kitchen tour with introductions.

"Yeah, I'm the new guy," he replied, without looking directly at Ezra, and trying to end the conversation before it could get started. He recognized the tone; they're the ones who can't wait to initiate you and to parade out all of their grievances in one breath. "And surely the most disgruntled employee here is the dishwasher," he thought to himself.

Despite the short and nondescript exchange, and Jaime's efforts to ignore him, there was a mutual curiosity, an instant attraction that comes without warning nor explanation. It wasn't the attraction of opposites, though on the outside they were.

Jaime was a tall, slender young man of twenty-six with dark waving hair, a mustache, and green eyes. He had grown up with the love and support from his parents that Ezra had never had, though from his childhood, he was every bit as confused. Jaime was born with a troubled heart. His mother would watch him through the window, as he sat between the two trees in their front yard, staring off towards the distant fields. He never seemed to belong. The other children would be playing games all around him while he sat alone, his mind arrested by an overwhelming darkness. It was this inner discord that he and Ezra had in common, and that had connected the two at a moment, and through a medium that had set its hands on Jaime at birth.

"It's all meaningless you know," Ezra called out. Jaime looked back at him a second time as he made his way to the front line to assume the position as head cook.

"Just ignore him," said John, shaking his head and sighing. "Look, Ezra's got problems, but he's here every day and he gets the job done. He won't give you any trouble. Just don't take what he says to heart," he said laughing, "it may make you crazy as he is!" John was the restaurant manager, and as usual, Jaime had already forgotten everyone's name, including his.

"I normally give him a ride home after work, but with you on board now, maybe you could give me a break?" John asked. "It's not too far from here, but at one in the morning, well, he's the best dishwasher I've had, and I don't need him disappearing on me."

"Sure Jim, I can do that," Jaime replied. John immediately corrected him, "It's John."

"Right, sorry," Jaime said under his breath. His eyes were locked on Ezra through a reflection in the small round window of the kitchen door.

That first night's shift dragged on like a preacher's prayer, but Jaime dispatched his soul and delivered a barely convincing performance of someone who actually cared about any of this.

Jill was fussin' at the world while mopping the grease-covered floor. The others were trekking through the kitchen and filing out the back exit.

"Get outta here," she hollered, "I can't go home 'til y'all get your dirty asses off my clean floor!" But despite her efforts, the floor never came clean and she knew it, but she could dispatch her soul, too.

Ezra timidly stuck his head inside the kitchen door. "That's good enough, Jill. I can't go home 'til you pretend this floor's clean. Jaime's my ride and he can't shut this place down with you still in it." Ezra pulled his head back, closing the door, and just escaping Jill's swipe at him with the mop.

Jaime had to cross the floor to get out the back exit and lock up, but he stood frozen with what to do. He was a little scared of Jill.

He peeked at her through the front door to the kitchen while Ezra peeked in at her through the back. Jill watched and waited for one of them to make a wrong move, but they both knew better. When she was finally done, she put the mop away, and signaled to Jaime. He skated his way across the now wet, greasy floor and turned the lights out behind him. With day one mercifully over, the regrets of leaving art school for this meaningless affliction took over his thoughts.

Already dreading tomorrow, he closed the door, leaving the moments he had to hide from his soul on the other side. It was one o'clock in the morning, and time to chase impossible dreams, but those would have to come after he had taken Ezra home.

Ezra adjusted himself into the close quarters of Jaime's small Volkswagen. He lit a cigarette, and without a word, pointed with his smoking hand and a tilt of his head towards the general direction that led them out of the restaurant parking lot and onto the main road.

"Where are we going?" Jaime asked, as he pulled a pint of vodka out from under his seat.

Ezra gave him a curious glance. "Aren'tcha a bit young to be leaning on that bottle?" He reached over and took it from his hand, turned it up, and passed it back.

Jaime shrugged his shoulders.

"Just follow this road out until it turns into two lanes and then hang a left after the tunnel. I'll show you from there."

Jaime knew where the tunnel was, and he also knew this road was leading them out of town. Sorting through the tapes scattered on the floor, Ezra helped himself to the music, and with a surprised look of approval, loaded the Youngbloods and stared out the window.

Neither said a word until the tunnel came into view. Turning left, and leaving the last of the city lights behind them, Jaime asked, "Where to now?" He was beginning to feel uneasy about where Ezra was leading him. "There are no houses out here," he thought to himself.

"Past this bend in the road. On the right, you'll see a small white building."

"Okay, I see it. Then where?"

"No, that's it."

"Wait. What? That's it?"

"What were you expecting?" Ezra asked under his breath.

Wishing he'd not asked that out loud, Jaime pulled in slowly alongside the building, his headlights shining through the nearby woods that lined the railroad tracks in the back. He sat for a moment while Ezra gathered his jacket and the food he'd brought home from work.

"You gotta be somewhere?" Ezra asked.

"No."

"You don't say much, do you? That's alright, come on."

Jaime turned the key, and everything went quiet and dark. He stepped out and watched as Ezra walked over and grabbed a flashlight from the floor just inside the doorway. He could hear Ezra talking to himself as he moved through the building lighting candles and incense. Wanting nothing more than to sleep, but feeling drawn to stay, Jaime hesitated for a moment, turned back to scan his surroundings one last time, and went inside.

"I see you wear a cross. You religious?" Ezra asked.

"Not really."

"Well, neither am I. Here, put this on your tongue, and let's go see if we can find this god I hear everybody talking about."

Jaime laid still on his back and unbuttoned his chest, carefully pulling the dark clouds out of his heart and arranging them in the sky that hung at arm's length above. They responded to his touch by swirling and spreading like dropping watercolors in a pool.

Ezra was absorbed in thought over his air mattress. As soon as he would disconnect the bicycle pump, it would lose what little air it had before he could close the valve. He would get up, examine the mattress thoroughly before sitting back down on it, and doing the same thing over and over again. He never seemed to get frustrated. Each time he would just tilt his head in curiosity, study the problem, and like Sisyphus, push the stone back up the mountain.

The ethereal strains of an electric guitar, incense, and cigarette smoke filled the room. There were no windows, but there was no door either, only an open threshold, where one once was.

The occasional breeze of the fresh night air would find its way in, cutting through the smoke and ruffling the flames on the candles. Without a word, they both carried on through the morning and into the afternoon, lost in their own lost worlds, until the LSD wore off and they drifted into a ragged sleep.

The sound of sirens rushing past the open doorway startled Jaime from his dreams. It was late in the afternoon and he was only a couple of hours away from having to return to work. Still in the clothes he'd worn the night before, he lifted himself, looked around the room, and began trying to recall the last fifteen hours, sorting the real from the rest. He'd been lying on the floor of an abandoned block building, situated only a few feet away from a secluded two-lane road outside of town. Noticing his shirt unbuttoned and his chest covered with marks, he looked over at Ezra who was asleep on a deflated mattress, holding the bicycle pump and using his work apron as a blanket.

The cinder block walls enclosed a featureless space of about forty feet squared, with a concrete floor and a ceiling so worn in places that the rain came through in full force. The missing door, and the candles Ezra had placed on scattered crates, provided the room with its only light. The pungent smell of garbage from the plastic bags in the corner had little way of escaping, and he remembered the incense that Ezra had burned last night not helping, but only adding to the difficulty of breathing. In the middle of the room, and between where he and Ezra were lying, was a metal folding chair and a well-used two drawer filing cabinet that held a few dishes and some assorted cooking utensils. On top of the cabinet, there was a propane stove that Ezra used to heat the canned goods he kept stacked in the corner opposite the garbage bags. And hanging from a perfectly centered nail on the back wall, like a chapel cross, was his eight-track tape player. On the far side of Ezra's mattress was a large, halfway closed canvas suitcase stuffed with his clothes. It was the one he'd been given by his parents years ago when they had told him to pack up and leave.

Jaime stood up, looked at his watch, and walked over to the doorway. All was quiet. Whatever the sirens had been chasing must be miles down the road. He turned back, weighing in his mind what he was seeing and remembering in broken strands the night before.

CHAPTER 3

About That Cross

During the slower periods, Jaime would leave the front line, wander towards the back, and pretend to help Ezra catch up on dishes.

"Jaime's always back there," Jill whispered to Sarah. "Wonder what they're up to?"

Jill and Sarah worked together on the food prep side of the kitchen, and they had a direct view to the dishwashing station.

"I don't know," Sarah said with a shrug.

"Well, there's somethin' goin' on."

"Just leave it alone Jill, everybody doesn't have to be up to something."

Jill dismissed Sarah with an eye roll and went back to work at the cutting board. But she couldn't let it go. "I bet it's drugs," she said under her breath.

"Leave it alone Jill."

They didn't talk much when Jaime would assume the role as co-dishwasher, but Ezra could disrupt his day with only a few words, and Jaime wanted disruption, something to derail him from becoming absorbed in the useless patterns of a useless day in what was beginning to feel like a useless life.

"Why do you wear that cross?" Ezra asked, handing him another plate to rinse.

Like nearly everyone else in that part of Appalachia, Jaime had grown up in a Christian family, living in a Christian-shaped environment, and being channeled into placing his faith in some grand purpose and eternal reward for good behavior. Christianity dominated the region's narratives and principles and was woven into the very fabric of every aspect of daily life. Everyone may not have been *devout*, but everyone was Christian.

Everyone except the dishwasher.

The day Jaime watched his mother being carried out in a box, was the day he dismissed it all. He was twelve years old, and not yet able to formulate in his mind, what at twenty-six he was coming to accept, that maybe life has no purpose or meaning, grand or otherwise. Maybe it's nothing more than a span of useless endeavors, random fortunes, or misfortunes, dictated by the whims of forces from beyond the veil, and outside our control. And there were days when he could feel these forces fast on his heels. And it was on those days that he seemed to be most drawn to rinse dishes.

"Is it superstition? You think it protects you from something?"

"Maybe," Jaime said as he glanced over at Jill, feeling her eyes on him. "I don't know."

"You got demons chasing you into a corner?" Ezra asked, as though he knew.

Jaime stared across the kitchen. Ezra was in his head, looking around and turning up secrets.

"When they catch you, they'll rip that cross off your neck and slice your heart open with it. And they'll be doing you a favor."

Jaime left the dishwashing station and went back to the restroom to be alone. With his hands bracing himself on the sink, he slowly lifted his head to see the ancient cross hanging from his neck. Covered in a dark patina, the bronze relic had been worn smooth and thin by the fearful but trusting hands of its past owners for centuries.

It had been left for him by his mother, who had placed it in a small jewelry box, only days before she died. With it, was a note that read, "This is the cross I held while praying over you each night as you slept. It belongs with you now as I will be gone soon. Wear it always, it will keep you safe, my darling boy." He cried as he strung it with her beads.

Her gravesite was only a couple of blocks off his morning route to school, and he would occasionally leave early enough to walk over with fresh flowers and to tell her how much he missed her, and how he wished they could have said goodbye. On one of these early mornings, he was met by a nun who was returning from the gardens and passing along the cemetery adjacent to the church grounds. The path was narrow and their speaking to one another was going to be unavoidable, which made Jaime uneasy. He didn't like having to say good morning to anyone, but especially a nun. They made him particularly uncomfortable.

Nuns could discern evil, and though he hadn't yet come to terms with its presence in his heart, there was a darkness that was wresting away his soul. It had found fertile ground in his vulnerable and lost nature as a child and would stir within him a terrible fear in the presence of the nuns. He approached her with his head down, trying to look invisible, while she, on the other hand, had watched him from afar, gladly anticipating their happy greetings.

"Good morning young man," she said as they came closer.

"Good morning, Sister."

"What beautiful flowers you have! May I look?"

Beginning to realize the worst, that he was going to be pulled into a conversation, he tried presenting them while not coming to a complete stop and hoping she would see that he was in a hurry. He wasn't of course, and it didn't work anyway, as she reached out to hold them while bringing her face in closer.

"Oh, they smell so lovely, God's wonders are new ev..."

She stopped and gently pulled the flowers away as she recognized the cross that hung around his neck. Placing her hand over her mouth, she stepped back and searched his face.

"You're him. I see it now. Your eyes. And you have the cross."

He looked at her with some hesitation and surprise. "I'm who? How do you know me?"

"What do you know about that cross you're wearing?" she asked.

"My mother gave it to me. Well, she left it for me. She's gone now. These flowers are for her. She's just over there."

"Yes, I know she is dear."

"She said she used to hold it when she would pray over me. How do you know me?"

She took his arm and led him over to a bench that sat beside the path.

"I gave that cross to your mother. I remember like it was yesterday, though it was years ago. You were only a young boy at the time. Your mother brought you to see the priest, and I attended the prayers. This cross..." she took it, lifting it from his chest with her trembling hand, "... I brought it back with me from my pilgrimage to the garden of Gethsemane. Do you know this place?"

"It's from the Bible," Jaime said.

"Yes, it is. It's where Jesus faced his terrible hour of decision. That night he sat alone with his tortured soul in the dark garden, waiting for the soldier's lights to expose him. I say alone, his friends were with him, but they were sleeping."

"They didn't know," Jaime said, coming to their defense.

"No, they didn't," she quickly replied. "I see you know this story. Then you'll know how it ends." She paused, crossed herself, and continued, "It was the night evil had its way."

"I have school, Sister," Jaime interrupted, as he rose from the bench. He wasn't sure what all of this had to do with the cross he wore, and no longer wanted to know. He didn't like thoughts of evil.

"School can wait child," Sister Anna said, gently taking his arm. "Please sit, we won't be long." Jaime slowly sat back down. "I was a young woman at the time of my pilgrimage and was struggling to keep at bay the demons that drove me there and ultimately to the convent. As I was sitting in the garden one day, alone and crying, an Armenian priest came and sat beside me, and with great pity and kindness, he listened as I spoke to him about things that people like you and I know."

She paused. "I realize you're still a child, but these things will come to you with age. Suffer with me for a few more moments. Armenia was one of the earliest of all the Christian civilizations, from a time when people still believed in the spiritual forces at war over our souls. These crosses weren't meant for decoration, they were meant for protection."

Jaime was staring at the ground in front of him, pushing the gravel around with his feet. The sister went silent and looked at him until he finally lifted his eyes towards her.

"This is the origin of that cross you wear, child. It has traveled a great distance and survived many centuries in coming to you. Your mother trusted its power over darkness. That's why she left it for you..." She looked into his eyes.

"Jaime."

"Yes, it's Jaime, I remember now. I'll be gone too someday, Jaime. Please listen."

He nodded, and she continued.

"As he prayed over me, he placed the cross that you wear in my hand, and closed my fingers around it, saying, 'Take this cross, it's protected many tortured souls for over five centuries, and it will protect yours as well. You will know when to pass it on.'"

"Why did you give it to my mother?" Jaime asked, with some concern. "What did she need protection from?"

"As I said, when your mother brought you to the priest that day, I attended the prayers over you. I listened while your mother told us of the dreams you were having. She believed them to be dreams, and I didn't want to cause her any greater fear than she already had by suggesting what I believed to be actual visitations. She said that you spoke about a man with a beak and a long tail who would come into your room at night and rub bad feelings into your chest."

Jaime sat paralyzed with fear as the images came flooding back into his mind. Images that had been suppressed and lain dormant for years. He jumped, startled by the sudden ringing of the church bells above them, and with his heart pounding, he stood up.

"I have to go, Sister!"

He started down the path in panic and fighting back tears.

"Wait!" she called out. "There is more to say."

"I can't, I have to go. Why did you tell me these things?" he shouted without looking back.

"You needed to know child," she replied, though he was already too far along to hear. "He may not be finished with his work," she said in a more somber voice, staring at the flowers that had fallen to the ground. Crossing herself once more, she picked them up and made her way over to the gravesite where Jaime's mother laid at rest.

With his heart pounding in his throat, Jaime ran along the path as far as he could before collapsing against a large hemlock tree, completely out of view of Sister Anna, the church, and the cemetery. Trying to catch his breath, he looked down and ripped the cross from his neck, and bitterly slung it across the path. Sitting with his head in his hands, sobbing and scared, he remembered his mother's words, "Wear it always, it will keep you safe, my darling boy." Lifting his head and blinking away the tears, he crawled over to where he'd thrown the cross and frantically sifted through the grass until he'd found it.

"I can restring it," he thought, and sliding it into his pocket, he took a deep quivering breath, and made his way towards the school.

Jill knocked on the restroom door. "Jaime? You alright in there? We're gettin' kinda busy out here."

He'd lost all sense of time while nervously pacing and smoking Ezra out of his head. He splashed his face with cold water and opened the door, releasing a room full of smoke ahead of him.

"I'm alright Jill," he said, squeezing through, between her and the wall on his way back to the front line.

Jill waited to see that he was gone and then stuck her head in through the restroom door, looking around with suspicion, and expecting to find some evidence of drug use. Satisfied for the moment, she began pulling the door closed when she saw in the mirror, written with soap, were the words, "I AM NOT FINISHED."

CHAPTER 4

I Took the Bait

Jaime stepped outside the back door of the restaurant, took his seat on the upside-down bucket that set against the wall, lit a cigarette, and looked up at the stars. His mind was a sacred place, and no one was allowed there. He never shared his inner thoughts with anyone. Although his countenance had always threatened to betray him, he managed to deflect questions like, "What's wrong?" with evasive enough answers that eventually led those who knew him to conclude that he just suffered from a natural despondency, and that if there were to be anything wrong, he wasn't likely to tell them.

The last garbage can came crashing through the door from the inside, swinging it open and breaking the silence, and his thoughts. "We're almost finished," Ezra said, while emptying the can into the dumpster.

Jaime looked up at him. "What?"

"We're almost done in there. You still taking me home?"

"Oh. Yeah, I'm taking you home."

Ezra reached down and slid the pack of cigarettes out from Jaime's shirt pocket, pulled one out, and sat down beside him.

Jaime hung his head, looked up at Ezra, and nervously asked, "Why do you live in that building?"

Ezra stared at the dumpster that was sitting behind Jaime. "My father owned a seed distribution business, and when he closed it down, he had the warehouse demolished, but left that small storage building standing."

"But why are you..."

"Listen man, I'm trying to tell you. My father's got a high profile. He runs the finance committee of a huge church, and he's a member of Fox Den, the largest social club in town, that's if you're not counting the church. He hangs out with city council members, the chief of police, the mayor, you name it." Ezra stood up and began taking his apron off. "But I got a high profile in this town, too." He folded the apron and placed it on his bucket, like a cushion, and sat back down. "Our profiles weren't compatible," he said with a bitter laugh. "Something, or someone, had to give. And it sure as hell wasn't gonna be him."

Ezra reached over and helped himself to another cigarette.

"It didn't use to be this way though," he said. "I remember back when I was thirteen, I got baptized, and was treated like the sun rose and set on me."

Jaime lit another cigarette. "You were baptized?"

"Yeah, this preacher tricked me." He looked down at the parking lot, shook his head, and then lifted it again with his jaws clenched. "So he says something like this Jesus had come to make all things new, and that god was at work restoring this shit for a world we live in."

He turned his head, "I took the bait."

Jaime watched him with empathy.

"Anyway, nothing's changed. I'm not accepting some life-sur-rendering dream that amounts to nothing more than club meetings on Sundays and trying to act respectable during the week. I mean, get this, my father's role in this new world order is the same as his business. Handle the money and try to make more."

Ezra stood back up and began pacing. "This dream's not sup-posed to be a better version of the same, or the best behavior humans can muster, or a seed business with a cross on it. Life is supposed to be, according to this book, the result of something otherly breaking in and transforming us from the inside-out."

Jaime was in church.

"This thing is supposed to be upsetting the momentum of the systems and structures that this Jesus had condemned. Instead, as far as I can see, the church only supports and reinforces these structures. Hell, sometimes they even give birth to them!"

Ezra abandoned all hope in finding some greater purpose in, or meaning to life, and with this parched dream burned and cleared away, his heart was now being cultivated for another campaign. An insidious darkness had taken up residency in his heart, and it was welcomed. It was the one thing that promised him nothing-only the truth.

"You know, I'd been better off if I'd never been lured into this lie, and then to have followed it down a dead-end road."

Jaime nodded his head. "The drugs?" he asked.

Ezra's head slightly trembled as he took a deep breath. "Yeah, the drugs. You gotta cope somehow. I notice you prefer the bottle. Like I said, though, you seem kinda young to be drinking like you do. What are you coping with?"

Jaime fixed his eyes on Ezra's and shrugged his shoulders.

Ezra's mother finished her tea and stared into the bottom of the cup. "But where's he gonna go?" She asked his father.

"I don't give a damn!" He can live in the woods for all I care. I want him out!"

"What about letting him stay in your storage space, at least for a while? I don't think it'll take long for him to come to his senses and straighten his life out."

"He's never gonna get his life straightened out, and you know that, Helen. But if it'll help ease your conscience then okay. I'll have to get it cleared out first, or he'll sell every damn thing I have in there to buy his drugs"

Her conscience wasn't exactly relieved, but she was feeling less like an accomplice to a crime. Helen walked over to the sink and started washing the dishes. Without looking up, she added, "You'll need to tell Captain Thomas, of course, or he'll run him off. I mean, it's your property, and as long as he has your permission to be there, they should leave him alone."

He closed his eyes and took a measured breath. "I'll tell him, but I'm not shielding him from his criminal activities. If they arrest him again, I don't care if he's on my property or not, he can rot in jail."

"Fair enough," she said, knowing she'd gotten the best deal he was going to offer.

Later that week, Helen dropped Ezra off at the small block building, his new home, she believed, until he learned his lesson and came back to his father's house filled with remorse and a commitment to change.

"You can always come back, you know, but you have to abide by our rules," she said to him, as he wrestled his suitcase from the backseat.

He paused from the struggle, and a sympathetic grin crept across his face. "Let's just finish this, mother," and he closed the door.

Jaime adjusted himself on the bucket.

Ezra leaned against the side of the building, took his cap off, and ran his hand through his hair. "By the time I was nineteen, my father had had enough of my trips to jail and threw me out. My mother talked him into letting me stay in that..."

Jill opened the back door. "We're done in here, no thanks to you two," she said, looking at them suspiciously.

Ezra and Jaime reluctantly put their cigarettes out and went back inside. Ezra to grab his jacket and the food he'd set aside for later, while Jaime began locking things up.

"What are you not finished with, Jaime?" Jill asked as she met him coming out of the office.

"What are you talking about?" Jaime replied, closing, and locking the door behind him.

"The message on the bathroom mirror. You wrote, 'I am not finished.'"

"I didn't write that. I still don't know what you're talking about."

She led him over to the bathroom door and opened it, but the message was gone. Jaime looked over at Jill, she shook her head and walked away. Just then, Jaime caught a glimpse in the mirror of what appeared to be the man with a beak from his childhood dreams, laughing to himself. He turned quickly to look, but it was only Ezra making his way to the back door.

"Jaime..."

"Jaime!" Terry's raised voice finally broke his stare. Terry was one of the front line cooks. He had been trying to get Jaime's attention to come help him with the last of the grease bins, which should've been emptied before the floor was mopped, but what did it matter, the place held a permanent coat of grease from ceiling to floor and on everything in between.

"You okay?" Terry asked.

"Yeah, I'm fine. Let's try and do this before Jill mops next time."

"Well, I needed help with this, and you and Ezra were gone and..."

"Okay, let's just finish this," Jaime cut him off, exhausted already from a conversation over something he really didn't care about, and his mind was still arrested by what he'd just seen, or thought he'd seen. They finished emptying the grease, skated their way across the wet floor and out the back door. Jaime dropped Ezra off that night with no intention of staying. He sat with the car running for a moment outside the small building until he saw the dull glow from the candles through the open doorway, and before he could change his mind, he drove off, leaving Ezra to tread through the darkness of his thoughts alone. He had his own thoughts to confront tonight.

Jaime rented half of a small shotgun house in one of the more depressed and neglected neighborhoods in town. His narrow space consisted of a kitchen, a bath, and two rooms. His small bed and the table that held a lamp, his books, and an ashtray made up his bedroom. The front room was empty, apart from an old worn sofa that had been left by the previous tenant. Each room had a window that he had covered with old blankets in place of curtains. He threw his keys on the counter next to the stove and counted off the seven paces it took him to reach the lamp by the bed. The landlord had divided what barely amounted to one house into two and separated the living spaces with an interior wall so thin that a sheet of paper would've provided as much privacy.

Jaime could hear Raymond's voice, the sound of his work boots tramping, and the thunder of fists against the wall. They come and go in waves. He turned the lamp on and sat on the edge of his bed. Slowly unscrewing the cap, he listened for her voice, wondering if she'd survive another night.

Lisa and Raymond were the tenants on the other side, and Raymond was as vile a human as Jaime had ever known. Every night Jaime would come home to the barrage of violence erupting on the other side of the wall, and Lisa was always the victim of the rage. There was no place for her to hide from him, and once he was no longer satisfied with beating on the walls, he'd start on her. One morning, after Raymond had left for work, Jaime walked across their shared front porch.

"Please don't say anything," Lisa pleaded from inside the chain-locked door.

"I could call the cops," Jaime said. "I can't let him keep doing this to you. I can see the marks from last night."

"Please, please don't do anything. You'll only make it worse," she pleaded in a whispered voice. "Now go, if he catches you here it'll be bad. He really doesn't like you.

She closed the door and bolted it. That was a couple of weeks earlier, and Jaime had only been home a few nights since then. He'd been staying most nights after work at Ezra's. The violence would be over soon, but he just couldn't listen any longer, so he grabbed his jacket and stepped out back.

Off of the main highway that crosses the river and leads south and out of town, there's a narrow road that winds its way through the isolated hollows of the foothills and terminating only god knows where. Jaime had found himself on this road by accidental necessity one early morning after work. On certain nights he would drive down, park on the shoulder of the highway, walk to the edge of the river and sit until sunrise. It was on one of these early mornings, while approaching the bridge, that he saw in his mirror, a police car pulling out from a side street and begin following close behind.

He always had a bottle with him, and on most mornings, he'd wait until he reached the river, but on others, like this one, he started early. Turning the music down, he drove on, past his pull off, and across the bridge. He continued for several miles until paranoia took the wheel and he started looking for the next turn off of the highway. It was onto this unlit nondescript road that he turned, knowing that if the police car made the same turn, he was only moments away from seeing the blue lights, but if not, he'd soon be on his way back to the river. Jaime pushed the bottle from between his legs and onto the floor and then slid it under his seat with his left heel. He was rehearsing in his mind the impending sobriety test when in his mirror he watched the police car pass the turnoff and continue harmlessly down the highway.

He waited, instinctively believing that fate was luring him into another one of its traps and that at any moment he'd see the police car return with lights flashing. The further he wandered down this dark road, however, the more at ease he began to feel. Now to find a place to turn around. Appalachian second-growth trees and rhododendron lined the road to his left, and the river followed its contours on his right. He crept his way further along until a bridge in the distance appeared in his headlights. The river was slowing and swelling into a deep pool before cascading down the hollow and into the darkness. It was at this pool that the road turned, and the bridge crossed over. On the far end, the ground was level and large enough to pull over and park. Jaime stepped out and walked back to the bridge and sat down on the edge. As his eyes began adjusting to the dark, he was able to make out the large pool below. He sorted and settled his thoughts, tossed a rock into the water, and managed to rise to his feet without tipping over and falling in after it. He turned the key and began his drive back into town but would return to this bridge the next day.

All was calm now, and the last hour had crowded the events from work beyond the reach of his mind. As he closed his eyes and thought about sleep, the sounds of a new struggle emerged from the other side of the wall. Raymond was now quenching the thirst for his male prerogative and abuse in another way. Evil was gaining momentum like a runaway train, but this demon, he knew, could be stopped.

Jaime turned out the light, closed his eyes, and made a plan.

CHAPTER 5

You Forgot the Duct Tape

Jaime felt around for his watch and dragged himself out of bed. He was late for work. He splashed cold water on his face and thought through the details of his plan for the night. He filled his empty vodka bottle with water and rummaged around the house gathering up the things he would need, including a plastic garbage bag, an extension cord, and a belt. He stuffed them into a small backpack and stood at the back door trying to think if he'd forgotten anything. "I'll pick up another bottle on the way into work, and my gloves should still be in the car," he thought. Slowly closing the back door, he walked over to the car, tossed his backpack in the passenger seat, raised the front hood just enough to see the spare tire, got in, and shifted into reverse. "It'll float," he thought. Jaime stopped the car, dug around in the glovebox for a screwdriver, got out, and opened the hood again. He looked up and down the street behind him, and then pressed the screwdriver into the valve stem, letting the air out.

That evening, everyone was excited for Sarah, as she had just announced her impending marriage. Everyone except Ezra. And although no one had made the connection, the change in his mood was noticeable. Actually, he never seemed to have a mood, he just drifted in, assumed his position at the dishwashing station, and went through the shift with numbness to everything around him. To John, this made him the ideal employee. He never had to start him up or calm him down. It was as though Ezra was just another component of a dishwashing mechanism that steadily hummed in the background. But tonight was different. He had a mood and John had taken notice, but rather than wading into Ezra's low-grade temper himself, he pulled Jaime aside the moment he walked through the door.

"I don't know what's up with Ezra tonight, but something's got him on edge. He's not himself. He's agitated about something, I don't know what, but you may want to check in on him. He seems to like you. Anyway, I've got to go. I've been waiting for you to get here. By the way, you do know your shift starts at five o'clock, right?"

"Yeah, sorry I'm late, I had some things I had to take care of. I'll go see what I can do."

"Well, do your best with him," John said. "I don't want him quitting. You have any idea how hard it is to hire someone who seems content with washing dishes? Ezra has no ambition to do anything more, and that's the way I like it."

Jaime shifted his look from Ezra to John and then to the floor, not wanting to deal with what he'd just heard. He had other things on his mind.

He took a deep breath. "I'll see what I can do, he repeated."

Jaime made his rounds through the kitchen, making sure everything was in order before assuming what felt like a forced march back to the dishwashing station. He had warned Ezra to stay out of his head, but he wasn't sure what to expect tonight. Ezra was visibly troubled. Jaime stopped short of the station and thought. He looked over at Mike, one of the busboys who was trying to impress a waitress by balancing a soup spoon on his forehead and called him over.

"Take the dishwashing for a few minutes, Mike, I need Ezra's help outside."

"Sure, boss."

"Don't call me that, please. Just cover him for a few minutes. We won't be long."

Jaime walked over to Ezra and asked him to step outside for a smoke. As they approached the back door, Sarah could be overheard talking with Jill.

"I can't believe it!" she said. "I'm finally gonna be married and then I'm gonna start a family, and..."

The back door closed behind them, and they took their seats on the buckets. Jaime handed Ezra a cigarette and thought about the vodka he'd bought on the way into work. "I'll be right back."

Pulling the bottle out of his backpack reminded him of the job he had to finish later that night. He pressed his forehead onto his arm, which rested across the top of the car. The images of the belt and the trash bag lingered as he closed the door. He took a long drink before walking back towards Ezra. Sitting down, he passed him the bottle and lit a cigarette.

"We can't drink it all, Ezra. I need it for later, and besides, we still have to function tonight."

Ezra took a drink and turned his head away.

"What's the point? It's all meaningless. Marriage, family, what's the point? Hasn't that all been done before? It's a meaningless cycle vomiting up another meaningless existence."

"I guess it's about love," Jaime said.

"Love!" Ezra snapped, throwing the bottle across the parking lot, grabbing Jaime by his collar and shoving him off the bucket and onto his back.

"Goddammit Ezra, get off of me! What the hell's the matter with you."

"What is love!" Ezra shouted through clenched jaws and spitting in Jaime's face. "Some useless drug that fools conjure up to convince themselves that they matter?"

Jaime stopped pressing and relaxed against the pavement. Ezra finally released his grip and crawled back onto his bucket.

"Fools! You don't matter, least of all to the one who said you did."

Jaime propped himself up on his elbows and watched as Ezra wiped his eyes. This was not one of his philosophical rants. Ezra was anguishing. He had let something slip out.

Several years before he was put out of his father's house, Ezra had fallen deeply in love with a girl he had gone to school with. He was consumed with her, and she with him. They were inseparable for nearly two years, and the darkness in his soul was having to make room for this growing warmth, this rest, this safe place. Everything was standing still. There was no past, no future, only every timeless moment with Celia. But his vulnerability had led him to take the bait, and the trap closed on him again.

While they were saying the things that lovers say, Celia left him for someone else. Her leaving had killed off what was left of his heart, and this time the darkness took back his soul in force. For Ezra, love was the hardest problem to solve. It isn't something that's conjured up, and he knew that. The bitterness that now consumed him was its own evidence. If love is something we create, then it can easily be dismissed. No heart would ever be broken if we could simply decide not to love anymore, and as hard as he tried, he could not drive his love for her away. He was ruined. The one thing that was dismissed, was the myth about broken hearts. Time doesn't heal; it only waits.

Jaime didn't know what to say. It was obvious that the subject of love had triggered something deep and painful within Ezra's past. He wasn't going to pull anything out of him, but Ezra wasn't going to say anymore anyway, and besides, he'd said too much already. Jaime had lost a young love too, but the closest thing to the brokenness that Ezra was feeling was the loss of his mother, and he knew that somehow it wasn't the same. He looked over at Ezra who was staring into the ground. This was new. He'd seen him troubled before but not like this. He looked utterly defeated. He finally picked himself up off the ground and set his bucket back in its place.

"Let me take you home, Ezra. You don't need to be here tonight."

Without saying a word, Ezra stood up and started walking to the car. Jaime took a step towards the back door thinking he'd let everyone know what he was doing, but then waved it off and followed, sighing at the broken vodka bottle that was strewn across the parking lot. Ezra got there before Jaime and grabbed his backpack out of the passenger seat, spilling its contents. He cut a knowing eye at Jaime while placing the curious items back inside the pack.

"You forgot the duct tape," he said casually, as he adjusted himself into the seat. Jaime froze with fear.

"That plastic bag's not soundproof, and you're probably not gonna want to hear him beg," Ezra continued.

Jaime went flush. His heart was pounding and moving up his throat. He stepped back out and braced himself against the car, struggling to regain some composure. He had the ability to think fast and cover his tracks, but not this time. It was all over. Whatever chance there may have been to explain it all away had passed and the longer he stood outside thinking about it, the more guilty he looked. There was nothing left to do but get back in the car and stubbornly pretend as though the last few minutes had never happened. He got in, closed the door, and pulled out of the parking lot.

"Mike can cover you," Jaime said. "He'll be behind all night, but I'll help him out." Ezra turned and locked his eyes on him with a look of cold disbelief. Jaime could feel his glare, but he wasn't going to give in. He was determined this show was going on whether Ezra agreed to play along or not, and he was going to see it through to the end. But that wouldn't be necessary. Ezra turned back towards the window and fought back tears, while Jaime's thoughts drifted towards the job ahead. Without another word, or even a thought for the other, they pulled up to the white cinderblock building, and Ezra got out of the car. They went their separate ways, each with their own work to do.

Ezra laid back on his mattress and remembered Celia. He rolled over, curled up in a fetal position, and sobbed.

Jaime returned to the restaurant and told Sarah he wasn't feeling well, and that he would need her to take over, close and lock up.

"I just need to grab a few things," he said.

Ezra reached over to Jaime's side of the filing cabinet and grabbed the bottle of vodka he'd left the last time he was there. As he rolled back over, he saw him in the doorway, snapping his beak. "Leave me alone! I'll do it. Just leave me alone!" he shouted through the tears.

Jaime snuck a bottle of vodka from the bar, to replace the one Ezra had flung across the parking lot and went into the storage room.

Ezra heard the train's whistle blowing in the distance.

Jaime looked across shelves and dug through boxes.

Ezra put his boots back on and finished the bottle.

Jaime found the duct tape and rushed out the back door. He needed to get back to his place before Raymond came home from work.

CHAPTER 6

Fingerprints

Jaime ran into the house and placed the vodka bottle filled with water, and the bottle he'd taken from the bar, in the cabinet above the sink. He marked the bottle filled with water by scratching off the corner of the label. He rummaged through the top drawer, grabbed a wrench, and ran outside to turn off the main water line. His heart was pounding. He ran back inside and turned the faucet on to empty the line and dove under the sink to disconnect the hose. Finding the rubber gasket, he chewed through the side of it with his teeth, breaking it apart and then placing it back and reconnecting the hose. He ran outside, turned on the main, ran back inside, threw the wrench in the drawer, and filled a saucepan with water. He dumped the pan under the sink, filled it again, and dumped it onto the kitchen floor. He threw a few towels on the floor, checked to be sure the hose under the sink was leaking and ran into the bedroom to write the note.

Raymond worked as a plumber's handyman, and Jaime was counting on Raymond's need for a few extra dollars, and the stroking of his male ego, by asking him to come over and have a look. He wrote down on the back of an envelope, "Raymond, my kitchen sink is leaking, can you come fix it? I'll pay you, Jaime." He slowly and carefully opened his front door, stepped out onto their shared porch, and as quietly as he could, opened Raymond's screen door and closed it onto the note.

Slipping back into his side of the duplex, he moved the blanket covering the front window to the side and watched to be sure that Lisa hadn't heard him and removed the note, as she would have. Darting his eyes up and down the street, that ran only feet along the front of the house, he looked once more at Raymond's door. Convinced that the bait was set, he let go of the blanket and began pacing the room, waiting for his knock at the door. He slumped onto the sofa to consider his resolve, but immediately stood back up to resume his pacing. Jaime started towards the kitchen sink to check it again when he heard the sound of boots on the front porch and froze in place. The screen door screeched open and Raymond knocked.

There he was, and the look on his face chased any remaining hesitation away.

"How much you gonna pay me for this?" he asked, shoving the note into Jaime's chest.

"Twenty bucks?" Jaime offered.

"Make it fifty," Raymond said, stepping past Jaime and intentionally clipping his shoulder.

Jaime glared at Raymond with disdain and satisfaction, as he made his way to the kitchen, knowing that he could've asked for a thousand dollars, it didn't matter, he was never gonna see a penny of it anyway.

Raymond got down on his knees and stuck his head under the sink. "Go turn the main off!" he shouted.

"I don't know how to do that," Jaime replied.

Raymond angled his face up and out towards him. "You really are a useless pretty boy, aintcha. Just find me a wrench. I'll go do it."

As soon as he was out the back door, Jaime ran into the bathroom and flushed the note down the toilet. He heard the tank stop filling. The main had been shut off, but the note was safely gone. He stepped back into the kitchen just as Raymond was stomping back in. He dropped to the floor, rolled over onto his back, and began disconnecting the fill hose.

"You want something to drink?" Jaime asked.

"What do you got?"

"I got vodka. Is that too strong for you?" He was purposely stoking and luring him into the trap.

Raymond slid his head out from under the sink. "Too strong for me? I drink that shit like water."

Jaime fought back a smile. "Yeah? So do I." He reached up into the cabinet and grabbed the marked bottle of water for himself and handed Raymond the bottle of vodka. "Here you go, try not to drink it too fast," he said.

"Just try and keep up you punk," Raymond said, before swallowing his first drink, along with the bait. The trap was closing, as Jaime matched Raymond's deep swigs of vodka, with water.

Raymond's inflated male ego took over, he wasn't gonna be outdone, and he drank too much, too fast. As was Jaime's plan. He tried setting his empty bottle out onto the kitchen floor, but he was already drunk, and it went rolling towards Jaime's feet.

"You need a new gasket," he slurred.

"Can we go get one tonight? There's a hardware store across the river that stays open late." Jaime knew that Raymond would be passing out soon, and he didn't want to have to carry his limp body out to the car.

"Yeah, whatever," Raymond mumbled, climbing out from under the sink, and staggering to his feet.

"Come on, I'll drive," Jaime said, hurriedly escorting Raymond out the back door and scanning his surroundings for anyone who might be watching. He helped him into his car and started towards the river.

"Raymond. Raymond!" Jaime was trying to stir him, but he was unconscious and slumped against the door.

"Good," he thought to himself.

It was already dark, no moon, no stars. A low hanging cover of clouds enveloped the valley. Jaime crossed the bridge and began looking for the turnoff. "There it is," he said under his breath. Checking his mirror, he made the turn too fast, throwing Raymond over the stick shift and into Jaime's lap. "God damn it!" He stopped the car in the road and pushed Raymond back over against the door.

"Where are we?" Raymond looked over at Jaime. "Where are we?" he repeated.

Raymond was still weak and on the threshold of consciousness, but Jaime couldn't take the chance of him waking up and having to put up a fight. He reached back and grabbed his backpack.

"Hey, where are we?" Raymond asked again.

Jaime ignored him and digging frantically through his pack, he pulled the extension cord out. Pushing Raymond's face against the window, he climbed up out of his seat and put his knee into the small of Raymond's back, holding him there while he grabbed one arm, wrapped the cord around his wrist, and then fought with him to surrender the other. Wrapping the cord around his other wrist and forcing the two together, he tied the knot and reached back into the pack for the duct tape.

"What are you doing, you motherfucker!" Raymond growled. He was fighting and struggling now to get loose. Jaime's heart was pounding, and his hands were shaking as he ripped off a stretch of tape with his teeth and covered Raymond's mouth, wrapping it all the way around the back of his neck. Raymond was fighting, kicking with his legs, trying to lunge at Jaime with his body, and butting at him with his head. His eyes wide open and his nostrils flaring as he snorted and grunted. Jaime was in a state of terror. This was not the plan. They were stopped in the middle of the road; what was he gonna do if a car approached. He had to finish this and get to the bridge. He ripped off another strip of tape and wrapped it around Raymond's eyes, he couldn't bear to look at them, and then noticed he'd forgotten to put his gloves on.

"Fuck it," he thought. It's too late now, surely the water will remove any fingerprints I might leave.

He grabbed the plastic bag and forced it over Raymond's frantically thrusting head and wrapped the belt around his neck. He started the car and sped off to the sounds of Raymond's grunts and his sucking the plastic in with his deep breaths. Flying down this narrow road and hugging the curves, begging to get there, he tried his best to keep pushing Raymond off of him with his shoulder.

"There it is!" he said out loud. "There it is!" he repeated with a cry of exhausted relief, as though they were both in this together. And they were until Raymond finally stopped his throws and slumped forward against the dashboard. Jaime looked over at him as he stopped on the bridge. Jumping out of the car, he ran to the front, opened the hood, and pulled the spare tire out. He ran around to the passenger door and opened it, guiding Raymond's limp body onto the bridge. He took the remainder of the cord he'd used to tie Raymond's hands, tied it to the tire, and pushed him over the edge and into the pool below. He stood with his chest heaving, watching, waiting, making sure that the body was submerged and was gonna stay that way.

Jaime leaned back against the side of the car as the rain began to fall. It was the same feeling he got from taking a shower. Not only was his body being cleansed, but so was his soul. He looked up and let the rain drench his face.

The train was rounding the bend. Ezra's boots crushed the leaves that covered the ground. He slowly walked through the trees until his flashlight found the tracks. He climbed the small ridge, threw his cigarette to the ground, and stepped in between the rails. The train's whistle called out like a thousand trumpets.

Its metal wheels screamed. Ezra raised his arm and covered his eyes from the blinding light.

Jaime was asleep when later that night, he was startled awake by a knock on the door. He reached over for his watch. It was one o'clock in the morning, and the knock came again. He slowly made his way to the front window and pulled the blanket aside very carefully, but there was no one there.

CHAPTER 7

Ezra Won't be Coming In

Jaime sensed a presence that woke him again from his sleep. He raised up onto his elbows to see someone sitting on the edge of the bed.

"Death's just a door isn't it?" Ezra asked, "and pushing someone through it must be as satisfying as stepping through yourself." He ran his hand across his beard, stretched his chin upwards, cupped his neck, and stared at the hole in the ceiling.

"I knocked last night, but you didn't answer." Ezra looked at Jaime. "You think you did Lisa a favor, don't you," he turned his head towards the kitchen, "but of course you only did Raymond one. Wanna do her a favor? Show her through the door too."

Jaime was drained. He arched his back and pressed the heels of his hands into his eyes. "What the hell are you doing in my house, Ezra? And how did you get in?" He grabbed his pillow to prop himself up. But Ezra was gone.

"Ezra!" Jaime shouted.

He fought and kicked his way out of the tangled sheets, fell out of the bed, and thrust his protesting body into the kitchen. Ezra wasn't there, but the water on the floor and Raymond's empty vodka bottle were. Jaime chased off the repulsive scenes from the duct-taped struggle and looked into the bathroom. Ezra was nowhere.

He walked back through the bedroom, grabbed his cigarettes from the bedside table, and then on into the unused room that separated his bedroom from the front door. He fell back against the wall and lowered himself onto the floor. Staring straight ahead, with his eyes unfocused, he lit a cigarette and tried to understand what had just happened.

He wanted to believe it was a dream, but that seemed impossible. "I was awake," he thought, "that was not a dream." He stretched and reached over for a coffee cup from the table beside the sofa to use as an ashtray. "But it wasn't real either. He's not here." Jaime stood up and began pacing. "What's between a dream and reality? I mean, how porous is that veil? That door?" he wondered. "And why is death the only way through?" His countenance sunk as he slowly looked over towards the edge of the bed and realized what all of this meant. "It's true," he said, in a solemn voice. "Sister Anna was right. He's not finish..." A knock at the door stunned him out of his thoughts. He looked over through the bedroom and at the kitchen floor.

Jaime lived in a neighborhood where a knock at the door was not irrelevant. It sure as hell wasn't Mormons, and it would most likely be the cops. It had only been hours since he'd left Raymond at the bottom of the river. He really didn't expect to get away with it, and he wasn't completely sure how much he cared, but "Surely to god I'm not found out already," he thought. His heart was pounding as he walked to the window. He carefully moved the blanket away, and reluctantly looked outside. It was Lisa. He took a deep breath to calm his mind, crushed his cigarette out, and opened the door.

"Jaime, where's Raymond? He didn't come home last night."

"He didn't come home?"

"No. I just wondered if you knew where he could be."

"Well, he left here late, Lisa. Said he was tired and was gonna go home and sleep, and that he'd finish the sink today. So, you're saying he never came home?"

Jaime was struggling. He hated lying to Lisa. Some people just don't deserve this, they've been lied to enough, and she was one of those people. But for the moment, he was left with no other choice. He wasn't ready to tell her what had really happened last night.

"He left out the back door Lisa, it was late, maybe around one o'clock. I thought he was going right home. He'd had some to drink, but I don't think he was so drunk as to wander off and get lost. I mean, we're right next to each other. He couldn't get lost."

"I saw you both leave in your car. Where'd you go?"

"We went to get a gasket for the pipes. The hardware store just across the river. It stays open late."

"Did you get it?" she asked.

"Why would she ask that?" he thought to himself. He hadn't prepared for this. They didn't get the gasket, and there was no one at the hardware store who would've been able to say that they were there. Because they weren't! Paranoia was taking over. "Does she suspect something? Why would she ask that?"

"Uh, no we didn't. We were, uh, wrong about the store hours. They had closed before we got there. You wanna come in?" he asked, hoping to change the subject.

"I'd like to, Jaime, but I don't need to be in your house when he comes home."

"Oh, he's not coming, I mean, he's not, I mean, you could always go out the back... But never mind, you're right."

Lisa folded her lips in and to one side, and shook her head. "He's probably in jail again. I hope he rots in there." She took a deep breath, exhaled, and started back across the porch towards her front door. "I hate him," she said under her breath.

Jaime's soul sunk into a familiar pool of guilt and shame. He slowly closed the door with new reasons to hate himself. He made his way through the bedroom, lit another cigarette, and went on into the kitchen. He was only about an hour away from having to leave for work. He looked over at the sink. The cabinet door underneath was still open from where Raymond had had his head buried underneath. He was going to have to replace the gasket and clean all of this up himself.

He went outside to turn the main back on, so he could clean up and use the bathroom, but as he splashed water on his face and ran a razor across his neck, he caught a glimpse of someone moving behind him in the mirror. He dropped the razor in the sink and ran towards the bedroom, the living room, and back towards the kitchen. No one was there. He sat down at the card table where he ate his meals and lowered his head into his folded arms. "I'm either going mad, or they're baiting me." His thoughts turned back to the razor at his neck. He lifted his head and began to connect the two. Dreams, demons, madness, or whatever else, he had to get to work and see the dishwasher. He threw on some clothes, skated across the water on the kitchen floor, bolted out the back door, and left for the restaurant, forgetting to turn the main water line back off.

John met Jaime as he pulled into the parking lot, his sleeves pushed up, his tie tucked in, and visibly upset.

"Ezra's not here! Do you know where he is? We're going through hell in there!"

"I'll run over to his place and check on him," Jaime replied. "I'll be back soon."

"Hurry!" John stomped like a spoiled child to the back door of the restaurant. "I don't wash dishes!"

Jaime looked back to see John banging on the door and calling out for Jill to let him in. He'd locked himself out. Under any other circumstance, he would have taken his time to return with Ezra. He loved the thought of John having to wash dishes, but he couldn't give a damn about John right now. With panic pounding in his chest, he lit a cigarette, reached under the seat for his bottle and pulled out of the parking lot.

Water was pouring onto the kitchen floor, John was sweating over the dishes, Lisa was looking in the refrigerator to see what she had to live on, Raymond was rising near the surface, and Jaime was on his hands and knees vomiting. He had seen the men in white coats placing the last of the body parts in bags and loading them into the back.

"Well? Is that it?" the one asked. "Did we get it all?"

"Yeah, that's it. We're finished," the other said. "I mean, I can't account for all the organs, but I think we got the rest. You got his head, right?"

"Yeah, it's got a smile on it though, you don't wanna look at it, trust me."

Jaime lifted himself with one knee, and then the other, and watched as they closed the doors and drove off. He ran his sleeve across his mouth and tried to gather himself. He managed to get to his feet and looked over at the doorway that had been boarded up with a "No Trespassing" sign nailed to it, turned, and walked back to his car. He collapsed into the driver's seat, reached underneath for his bottle, lit a cigarette, and tried to imagine Ezra's final hour.

He stared out through the front windshield at the tree line that hid the railroad tracks from view, and shuttered, as he fought back the images of Ezra's final seconds. He opened his eyes, crushed his cigarette out, and slowly pushed the gear stick into reverse. There was no going back to the restaurant, not now. He backed out, and about half a mile down the road, he pulled over at a gas station to use the payphone.

"John! The office phone is ringing off the hook, are you gonna answer it?" Jill hollered.

"Can you not see that I'm up to my elbows here!" John wailed.

Jill stormed into the office, "Hello?"

"Hello? Jill? It's Jaime." He was having to shout over the passing traffic.

"Jaime? Where are you? "

"Never mind that. Tell John that Ezra won't be coming in."

"Wait, what? Why not? We need him, Jaime!" Jill lowered her tone, "John's driving us crazy. I'm gonna lose my mind in a minute."

"Just tell him, Jill. I'm not coming in tonight either. Actually, I won't be back at all. You can tell him not to call me too. Take care of yourself, Jill." He hung the phone up and walked back to his car.

Jaime slowed and waited for her to cross the street. The young girl rode her bike all over the neighborhood, and always waved at Jaime. Except today. Today she passed by, cut her eyes at him, and laughed. He stopped short his wave back and narrowed his eyes as she pedaled away. He was too dead inside to think about why she seemed different. He pulled in, opened the back door, and kicked aside Raymond's vodka bottle. He took his boots off, locked the door behind him, waded through the kitchen and into the bedroom where he passed out.

CHAPTER 8

I'll Get You Out of Here Soon

Lisa watched as Jaime poured ketchup over his scrambled eggs. "My father wasn't a bad man. It's just that we were poor, and it made him angry, so he'd drink. But that only made things worse. Whoever was nearest to him at the time, well, you know."

"Is that why you left?" Jaime asked, passing the ketchup.

Lisa immediately pushed the bottle away, looking at Jaime's plate and then at him with wincing disapproval.

"No thank you," she said, "and yeah, that's one of the reasons I left. I love my father, but..." Lisa couldn't finish her thought. "Are you really gonna eat that?"

Jaime had spent the last two days in bed, wrapped up in his blankets, and waiting for last week's transgressions to evaporate from his conscience. He hadn't mourned Ezra's death as much as he had mourned the loss of another measure of innocence. Forcing Raymond to the bottom of the river was like a shift at work, watching Ezra being collected into bags was sickening, but lying to Lisa was a sin. Not in a biblical, but in an immanent sense. Crimes he could justify, and gore could be reduced to blood and tissue, but lying to Lisa seared his soul.

Into his third day, he came out from his covers and ventured onto the front porch and into the sunlight. Lisa heard his screen door close and came outside. She sat down on the floor of the porch beside him, and they each waited for the other to say something.

"You hungry?" Jaime asked.

"Yeah."

He climbed to his feet and reached for Lisa's hand to help her up. "Come on, I'll make some breakfast."

Almost a year had passed since the morning Lisa quietly closed the door to her father's house behind her. It was 1969, and in metropolitan cities and on campuses across the country, new challenges to the suppression of women's rights had been gaining momentum. But Lisa, like most other young women living in small towns and rural areas, remained unaware and sheltered under male-dominated norms. University was for the rich white kids over in Albuquerque, not for Native American kids living on the outskirts of Santa Fe. But one didn't need to be aware of the movement, to be aware that something wasn't right. And she knew it and felt it on both a psychological and physical level.

With her elbows on the table, Lisa clasped her hands together and rested her forehead onto them as Jaime took his first bite. She couldn't watch. "Je ne peux pas," she said under her breath.

"You speak French?" Jaime asked.

Lisa raised her head. He wasn't supposed to hear that. "Yeah, it just comes out sometimes."

"What did you say just then?"

"Uh... I said these eggs look good."

"I hope you like them. Did you study it in school?"

"No. There was this old woman who lived at the end of our road. She paid me two dollars a day to come to her house in the afternoons and clean and cook for her. I would hear her talking to herself sometimes in French. I loved the way it sounded. Well, anyway, she ended up teaching me. Mainly just common phrases, but after a while, I got good enough to have simple conversations with her."

Jaime salted his eggs again. "I think it's nice."

"Yeah. She's probably the reason I'm here."

"What do you mean? I thought it was because of your father?"

"He was part of it, but one afternoon I was getting ready to leave, I'd finished my work, and as she handed me my money, she smiled and said that one day soon I'd get to do all of this for free. *For my husband.*"

Jaime put his fork down and listened closely.

"I guess I'd always known that's what happens, you get married and you cook, clean, and make your husband happy. But that day I went home feeling empty. I like to cook, and I don't mind cleaning, but spending the rest of my life doing it for a man? I mean, like's it's my job?" Lisa stared into the bottom of her glass. "If I ever fall in love, I want us to do everything together. You know?"

Jaime's eyes were empathetically locked on Lisa. "Yeah, I know. I watched my mother work like a hired hand."

"Well, that was it. I wasn't gonna do that, so one morning I went into my sister's room, kissed her on her forehead, and left her a note, telling her everything, and that I'd write her soon, and not to worry about me. I took fifty dollars out of my father's wallet, most of it was mine anyway, and quietly walked out the front door."

"You got here on fifty dollars?"

"No. The morning I left, I grabbed all I could fit into a bag and a backpack and walked for miles until I was picked up by a truck driver. I offered him the fifty dollars if he'd take me as far away as he could. He dropped me off in Oklahoma City, but told me to keep my money, he was glad to help."

Jaime lit a cigarette. "Do you mind?"

"No, go ahead, I don't mind."

Lisa took her glass over to the sink for some more water. "I was scared to death. I'm still scared, but I knew Oklahoma City wasn't far enough away, so I went to the bus station and asked where I could go for fifty dollars, and this was one of the places. I didn't want to go further south, and I don't like the cold, so I decided to keep going east. The woman at the counter said she'd been here before, and that the mountains were pretty, and the people seemed nice."

Lisa met Raymond at the homeless shelter the night she'd gotten off the bus in this quiet East Tennessee town. Twenty-one years old, and scared, she used him to protect her while she tried to figure out, "what now?" And he did, but it wasn't out of any genuine kindness. He guarded her like he did his tools, just another possession. She didn't really care though, as long as he shielded her from anyone worse than him. Within a few months, Raymond had managed to earn enough as a plumber's assistant to put down a rental deposit on the space next to Jaime's. Lisa was left with a decision, stay at the mission, or go with Raymond. She would come to regret the one she made.

"I don't know what to do now that Raymond's gone, though. You're the only other person I know in this town. Raymond didn't like me leaving the house. I don't know where he could be, or if he's ever coming back."

"But why would you let yourself be held hostage by him? I mean, you seem so strong and confident. I don't understand Lisa."

"I wasn't so much a hostage of *his*, Jaime, as much as I've been a hostage to fear. And it's paralyzed me." Lisa sat back down.

"I'm sorry, I shouldn't have said that."

"It's okay Jaime, you're a man, you wouldn't know what it's like."

They both looked away.

"My sister got out too, she lives in Albuquerque now."

"And your mother?" Jaime asked.

"I don't remember my mother. She died when I was young. All I have are a few photos. My older sister raised me and took care of me."

Lisa looked down at her plate, and then out the window. A tear ran down her cheek.

"I truly believed things would have turned out differently for me," she laughed bitterly, as she dried her eyes and pushed the food around on her plate. "My sister used to read me this book at bedtime. It was about these old women, they were sisters, and they would weave your life into a beautiful story. You couldn't see them, but they were always at work. I used to fall asleep at night dreaming about what my story was gonna look like, and my sister would remind me of this whenever I was feeling scared, mostly of my father. She said they were weaving my story into a safe and happy one. I wanted to believe it, and so I guess I did."

Lisa fought back the tears and said laughing, "I think those sisters forgot about me."

Jaime was locked in a helpless stare as he listened. He wasn't in a position to offer any encouragement and couldn't bring himself to lie to her again by suggesting that everything was gonna be alright. He hated people telling him that everything, "was gonna be alright."

"You wanna go to her?" Jaime asked. "Your sister?"

"Yeah, I would, but I don't have the money."

"I could send you there."

"Your coffee's too strong." She walked over to the sink to pour it out. "Could you really do that?"

"Of course. I can go in the morning and look at some days and times."

"Your sink works now?" she asked.

"Yeah."

"I guess I should go back home," Lisa said, looking through Jaime's bedroom and at the front door. "I hate being by myself."

"Stay here tonight. You don't have to be by yourself."

"Where would I sleep?"

"Sleep over there, in my bed. We can share the space. You can trust me."

Lisa felt safe with Jaime and was beginning to have second thoughts about going to her sister. She looked over into the bedroom and then again at Jaime.

"That sofa in the front room, I could just sleep there."

"No!" Jaime said. "I'll sleep there. You can have the bed."

"Either way, it doesn't matter to me," she said, as she collected the plates and cups.

"This isn't your job," Jaime said, rising immediately from the table and grabbing the dishes away from Lisa's hands. "Remember? Now go and get your things together, stay here tonight, and I'll look into a bus for you to Albuquerque in the morning."

Lisa hesitated, and then started towards the front door.

"Thanks Jaime. I'll be back tonight if that's okay."

"Yeah, just come on in. I won't be doing anything." He set the dishes on the counter and began filling the sink.

Lisa closed the front door behind her, while Jaime looked down at the kitchen floor that was still pooled with water from the night before. Reflecting back at him was Raymond's duct-taped face. Jaime shuttered. With his hands trembling, he turned the faucet off and reached for his vodka from the cabinet above.

Dishwashing could wait. He drifted into the front room, collapsed onto the sofa and into a state of remove.

Night came and Jaime was in a deep sleep when Lisa knocked on the door. No answer. She knocked louder, but there was still no answer. She looked in through the glass pane of the front door and could see Jaime asleep on the sofa. She bit on her thumbnail and thought about what to do. After a few moments of indecision, she let herself in, and gently placed her hand on Jaime's shoulder, nudging him awake.

"I'm here," she whispered. "Are you still okay with this? I'm scared to be by myself."

Jaime rolled over. "Lisa."

Lisa sat down beside him.

"You okay?" she asked.

"Yeah, I'm alright. You ready for bed?"

"I am. You sure you're okay? You look sad."

"Yeah, I'm okay, just tired. Come on, I've made the bed for you."

Jaime took Lisa by the hand and led her into the next room.

"It's a narrow bed, but it's comfortable enough, and I'll be in the next room if you need anything."

"Thank you, Jaime. I'll try not to wake you again. Thank you so much."

"You're welcome, Lisa." Jaime turned the lights out and felt his way back to the sofa.

Late into the night, Lisa awoke to the sounds of something moving around in the ceiling above her. There was a missing tile in the bedroom ceiling, and as she called out, she thought she saw her breath crystalizing in a frost vapor. Jaime was lying on the sofa, smoking a cigarette when he heard his name. He put his cigarette out on the dish below him and rushed to the side of the bed.

"You okay?"

"No, I thought I heard something in the ceiling. It was probably a dream, but it's got me scared. Would you mind sleeping in here with me?"

"No, I don't mind."

Jaime got into bed and looked up at the ceiling where the tile was missing. Lisa rolled over and buried her face into his neck. He put his arm around her and pulled her closer.

"I'll get you out of here soon," he said.

"Thank you, Jaime," and she fell asleep.

Jaime had been awake most of the night. He could see sunlight finding its way through the holes in the blankets that covered the windows. Reaching for his watch, he saw that it was well past eight. He looked over at Lisa before quietly easing out of bed. Seeing her sleeping so peacefully warmed his heart. He went into the kitchen and put some coffee on, lit a cigarette, and waited. He looked back into the bedroom and had second thoughts of letting her go, but that wasn't his decision to make. He found a pencil in the drawer and wrote a short note on a napkin, "Gone to check on bus tickets, be back soon." He laid it on his side of the bed and quietly closed the door behind him.

There was a bus to Oklahoma City, with a connection to Albuquerque, leaving on Thursday morning. Jaime thanked the clerk and sat outside on the pavement to have a smoke and imagine the what ifs. Reluctantly climbing to his feet, he started back towards his car which was parked a few blocks away. Rounding the corner on Broad Street, he passed a small market with a sign in the window reading, "Help Wanted." He stopped, pulled his jacket up around him and against the wind, and stared at the bridges crisscrossing above him. "I gotta have a job I guess." He opened the door and stepped inside.

"Can I help you?"

Jaime looked up from the floor and into her listless mocha-colored eyes. "Uh, yeah. I'm here about the job. Who do I see?"

"Just show up tomorrow," she said. "Honestly, the man that owns this shop is just that desperate."

Jaime looked around. "What's he pay?"

"A dollar seventy-five an hour."

Jaime looked away with despair. He thought of Lisa and the cost of getting her to New Mexico.

"Okay, I'll be back in the morning, uh…"

"Jasmine, my name's Jasmine."

"Thanks, Jasmine." And he turned towards the door.

"Oh, and I'm Jaime," he said looking back. "You're not from here, are you?"

"Why do you say that?

"Your accent's different. I mean, it's nice, though."

Jasmine smiled. "Yeah, I'm from Memphis."

"What brought you here?"

"Let's just say I'm on a break. Memphis is intense, and I'll be going back, but I need to be in a quiet town for a while. You know, a little self-care."

Jaime looked at Jasmine with a curious admiration.

"What?" she asked with a laugh.

"Nothing. I just never..." Jaime was watching a woman slip a box of crackerjacks into her pocket. Their eyes met, and she turned her head in shame. Jaime smiled and turned back towards Jasmine.

"I'll be here in the morning," he said, and left the shop with a new plan. Looking back, he motioned with his head for the woman to follow him out.

He waited on the sidewalk. She nervously stepped out and walked over to him as he pulled out what money he had in his pocket and handed it to her. "Take this and get whatever you can with it. Come back in the morning and I'll make sure you have whatever else you need."

"Thank you."

"It's Jaime," he said.

"God bless you, Jaime."

She reached for his hand.

"I'm Mary."

CHAPTER 9

Je T'aime

It was late November, and the rain was beginning to come more often. Jaime liked these days, dark and overcast with weeping clouds enshrouding the leafless trees. The world was moving further away from the light, as Jaime's soul had been doing for some years now. It was as if his life was bleeding out and filling the universe. A glass of water to an ocean.

As he made his way home, he thought of the river, and the streams that were feeding into it, and how the rain would cause them to swell. He wondered if or when the body would surface. He remembered the struggle in the front seat, but before any doubt could set in, he also remembered the sounds through the walls at night of Lisa struggling from the hands of that monster. He pulled on the handbrake, cut the engine off, and looked up at the kitchen window where Lisa had pulled the blanket away and was motioning for him to come in. Jaime rested his forehead against the steering wheel and took a deep breath. He turned and cut his eyes towards the passenger seat. "Never again," he said, as he pulled his jacket in close, and then ran through the rain to the door that opened for him as he reached it.

"I made breakfast," Lisa said. "Get in here before it gets cold!"

Jaime stepped in and noticed the kitchen floor was nearly dry.

"I mopped up most of the water, be careful though, it's still wet."

"You shouldn't have done this, Lisa!"

"I wanted to. You've been so nice to me."

"Yeah, but..."

"Anyway," as she covered his mouth with her hand, "I had some vegetables at my place, so I made you an omelet. I hope you like it."

Jaime walked over to the refrigerator and reached for the ketchup. Feeling Lisa's eyes on him, he slowly put it back and sat down.

"Thank you, Jaime," she said, tilting her head with a smile. "Here, if you gotta have something, use this." She handed him the saltshaker. "You seem to like salt. Just go easy with it."

Lisa poured Jaime a cup of coffee and sat down beside him. "So, what did you find out?"

"Well, I found a bus that leaves on Thursday. Is that too soon?"

"No, I don't think so. I don't have much to pack. Mainly my clothes."

"Hey, let's go to the laundromat after breakfast."

"Oh, Jaime, are you sure? I could get all my clothes clean. That would be wonderful! And don't worry, I'm gonna pay you back for everything."

"No, you're not."

"Well, we'll just see about that." Lisa finished her coffee, jumped up, and started collecting the dishes, but Jaime wouldn't turn loose of his. "I'll clean up, you've worked hard this morning, and besides, it's not your job. We're in this togeth…" He stopped himself. "Breakfast was wonderful Lisa, now you go get your clothes."

Lisa blushed, curtsied with a laugh, and started towards the door.

"Oh, and Lisa…"

"Yes?"

"You're adorable, but do you mind bringing my pajamas back."

"Sorry, Jaime." Lisa went weak with laughter. "They looked so comfy though, and I was cold this morning. I promise to bring them back!"

Lisa was always the scared and often bruised face speaking to Jaime with a guarded voice from behind a chain-locked door. And although he didn't believe in an afterlife, when Jaime heard her singing through the wall, he would have loved nothing more than for Raymond to be listening from the fires of hell.

Jaime and Lisa spent the afternoon on plastic chairs at the laundromat. They were watching people, side-eyeing one another, and laughing under their breath.

"People are strange," Jaime whispered.

Lisa laughed. "They are. Good thing we're not though, right?"

Jaime was hypnotized by the clothes spinning 'round.

"I mean, I bet some of these folks even pour ketchup on their..."

Jaime broke the stare with a roll of his eyes. Lisa laughed, "I'm joking, not really though. I mean, if ketchup's the worst you got..." she was interrupted by a man in front of them trying to put a dollar bill into the coin acceptor. They buried their faces into each other's shoulders. "Yeah, if ketchup's the worst you got."

"Shut up, Lisa," Jaime said laughing and rocking his head into her neck. "And I'm making dinner tonight."

"Oh yeah?"

"Yeah."

"What are you making?"

"Fish and chips, is that okay?"

She pulled her face out from his neck. "Yes! I knew you were English. It's okay though, I still like you."

Jaime rolled his eyes again and shook his head. "How long must I..." Lisa patted his shoulder. "Poor baby," she said. "Do you pour ketchup on your..."

Jaime dragged his hands down the sides of his face. "No! Salt and vinegar. Are you gonna recoil at the sight of that too?"

Lisa shrugged her shoulders; they laughed and showed the man how to use the bill accepter.

The afternoon flew by. Jaime had made dinner, and he and Lisa were washing the dishes together.

"I still wonder where he is," Lisa said, pausing and staring into the sink. "I mean, he didn't take anything. I don't get it. I keep expecting him to come back. I just hope I get out of here before he does."

Jaime's heart was hurting.

Lisa grabbed the next plate from the water. "Honestly, I don't miss him though. These last couple of days have been really nice, Jaime. You're different. You're sweet. It's like you're not a man at all, well, not a typical man, if you know what I mean. I feel safe with you."

Jaime nodded. "I know what you mean. I never really felt like I belonged, anyway. I got beat up a lot too. Boys at school would hold me down and..."

"Stop Jaime. Don't say anymore. I don't want to picture that."

Jaime pulled the stopper from the sink. "I don't miss him either," he said. "I didn't like him."

"He really, really didn't like you. He once told me he was gonna kill you 'cause he thought you and I were seeing each other while he was at work. That's why he would lose his temper sometimes."

Jaime grabbed the edge of the sink, straightened his arms, and hung his head. "I'm sorry Lisa."

She reached for the dishtowel, dried her hand, and ran it through the back of his hair. "It's okay Jaime, it wasn't your fault. You tried to help me. I was just too scared to let you."

"I understand."

"And I was foolishly thinking someday he would stop being so mean to me."

Jaime walked over and looked out the window. "Did you love him?"

"No, Jaime, I didn't. Not at all."

Time was standing still.

Lisa broke the silence. "Hey, that's the last of it. Don't give up, you're gonna make a great dishwasher someday," she said with a laugh.

Jaime turned and looked at Lisa. "What?"

"I'm joking. Now come over here, have a cigarette, and relax. I'll pour you a vodka. Drink it from a glass though, I want you to be present tonight."

Jaime was lost in thought.

"Come on," she insisted, handing him his cigarettes. "You relax, and I'm gonna go change into your pajamas," she said with a smile. "Can I put a record on? I like your music."

"Yeah."

"*Moon River*?" Lisa asked.

Jaime slid down onto the floor. "What is it about that song?"

"I don't know. I like it too, though. I think it..." A piece of Jaime's mail caught Lisa's eye as she was reaching for his lighter, and she smiled.

"It's French."

Jaime looked up. "What?"

"Your name, I just saw the spelling of your name."

Jaime turned his head. "Yeah, that was my mother."

Lisa handed him his lighter and turned towards the bedroom. "Je t'aime," she said under her breath.

With his back pressed against the wall, and his arms resting on his knees, Jaime loosely held the glass of vodka in one hand and his cigarette in the other. He wanted Lisa to stay, but he was afraid to say anything.

In the other room, Lisa held Jaime's shirt to her face and was beginning to hope he would ask her to stay, but she was afraid to say anything. She put his shirt on and wondered what to do. She walked over to the record player and lowered the needle onto the song she liked the most. She laid down on the bed and closed her eyes. No one had ever said, "I love you," to her.

She thought of Jaime and went back into the kitchen to check on him.

"Hey, get off the floor," she said with a laugh. "Wanna go for a walk around the block?"

"A walk?" Jaime asked, "around the block?"

"Yeah, a walk, around the block." She looked down at him with a sympathetic laugh. "We can get some fresh air, come on."

"Fresh air?"

Lisa put her hands on her hips.

Jaime wasn't getting out of this, "Uh, okay."

"And get your jacket, it might be chilly."

Jaime searched his mind for a reason why people went for walks, and then slowly lifted himself off the floor.

They stepped out onto the front porch, and the young girl peddled by on her bicycle. She turned back at Jaime laughing, and shouted, "He said to tell you he's not finished!"

Jaime froze. "I don't know what that was about."

"What what was about?" Lisa asked.

"That girl, I don't know what she meant by that."

"What girl?" Lisa asked.

"The girl on the bike."

"What girl on a bike? What are you talking about, Jaime?"

"Nothing. I mean, I don't know."

Lisa looked up and down the road, and then over at Jaime. "Here, let's get you back inside. Maybe this was a bad idea."

Lisa closed and locked the door behind them and sat down on the edge of the bed with him.

She reached over and took his hand. "Do you wanna talk about it?"

Jaime hesitated, looked away in shame, and said in an emotionless voice, "Sometimes I see things."

Lisa squeezed his hand. "What things?"

"People. I guess I see people."

Jaime stood up. "I'm alright, though. You don't have to stay tonight. I wouldn't blame you."

"No. You're not alright, Jaime, but I can tell you don't wanna talk about it, and that's okay. I'm here when you're ready. And I'm gonna stay, if that's alright, you don't need to be alone. And I'm worried about you."

He sat back down. "I'd like you to stay. It's been really nice having you here. You don't gotta worry, though. I'll make sure you're safe."

She reached over and brushed his hair over his ear. "I know you will. Wanna try and sleep? You look tired."

"Yeah, that sounds good."

Jaime went into the kitchen while Lisa changed into his pajamas and then waited for her to get into bed before turning out the lights.

"I can't see it in the dark, but I don't like that hole in the ceiling, Jaime. Can I come over?"

Jaime lifted the blankets and pulled Lisa over. She wrapped her arm around his waist and snuggled her face into his neck. Jaime pulled her in closer. She was warm.

"Jaime."

"Lisa?"

"Have you ever been in love?"

"Yeah, once. At least, I think it was love. She absolutely arrested my heart. We were just kids, I guess, but I know there was something real between us. I'm not sure love cares about how young or old we are. Have you?"

He felt her head shaking into his neck. "I'd like to be. I think, I mean, it seems like it'd be a nice thing if the person you loved, loved you too."

Lisa rolled over onto her back. "Maybe someday."

"It's nice until it ends," Jaime said, as he pulled the covers up to his neck.

"Does it end?" Lisa asked.

"No. Actually, it doesn't, and that's the problem. You're left wishing it would and wondering why they went away. I mean, how could they just, did they never really feel, was it all just a…"

Lisa snuggled back in and put her hand over his mouth. "It's okay, we don't have to talk about it."

Jaime sighed and brushed her hair from her face.

They were falling in love and yet both naively oblivious to it all. Neither wanted to be the one to mistake the other's kindness as anything more than just that. So they kept quiet about it and eventually drifted off to sleep.

The morning light broke through the holes in the blanket that covered the window. Jaime stretched and opened his eyes to see Ezra crawling back into the ceiling through the missing tile.

"Ezra!" He jumped out of bed, ripped the blanket away from the window, and looked up into the ceiling. "Ezra!"

Lisa raised up. "Jaime! What's the matter?"

"Nothing Lisa... I'm sorry, just a bad dream. I'm sorry if I scared you."

Lisa was scared for him, she knew it was more than a dream, but she didn't want to press him. "It's okay." Lisa squinted at Jaime's watch on the bedside table. "I guess we need to be getting up anyway. I didn't realize it was after nine. The bus leaves at noon."

Jaime went into the kitchen, lit a cigarette, and sat down on the floor. His hands were trembling. Through the night, Jaime had thought about asking Lisa to stay, but now he couldn't. "I don't know what's real and what's not."

"Who are you talking to?" Lisa was standing in the doorway. "You okay?"

"Yeah, I'm okay, sorry."

"You're not okay, Jaime. You're trembling. What's the matter? Who were you talking to?"

"Just a bad dream. I'm fine."

Lisa looked at him until he reluctantly made eye contact. "You don't *have* to tell me Jaime, but the bad dream cover's running out of gas. I'll put some coffee on."

While Jaime was waiting for the coffee to finish, Lisa went into the bedroom and quickly grabbed his shirt from her side of the bed. And with her eyes on the doorway, she stuffed it into her backpack and zipped it up as Jaime walked in.

He reached for her bags. "I'll take these out for you."

"I'm holding on to this one," she said, clutching the backpack against her chest.

"Okay, and I've got some money for you. For the journey."

"No, Jaime! You've done enough. You're not giving me any money. I'll be fine."

Jaime shook his head. "Well, at least go make yourself a couple of sandwiches. You're gonna be hungry, Lisa."

"Okay, I guess you're right."

Lisa went into the kitchen, and Jaime unzipped her bag to tuck the money inside when he saw his shirt. He looked back towards the kitchen. His heart sank, but there was nothing he could do about it. As much as he wanted to, how could he ask her to stay when he couldn't be sure that the demons chasing him wouldn't harm her too. He felt his heart breaking as she followed him out to the car. She got in and stared down at the floor between her feet. Lisa had never known what a breaking heart felt like, until now.

The parking garage across from the bus station was small with a low ceiling and support pillars running down the center that left just enough room for cars to get in and out. Jaime parked at the entrance and waited for the driver who was on his third attempt. They watched and waited. After several tries, he finally solved the problem and squeezed past them. Jaime pulled in and they both got out.

In the far dark corner was a crumpled figure wrapped in a blanket. Lisa followed Jaime as he walked over to hand him the cash he was digging out from his pocket.

"I'm Jaime. This is my friend Lisa," he said, as he placed ten dollars in the man's outreached hand. Lisa stood to Jaime's side, wrapped his arm in hers, and watched with curiosity.

"You shouldn't do that!" a woman called out from across the garage. "These drunks hole up in here and do nothing but drink all day and then ask people for money so they can drink more."

"Bombay. That's what my friends call me," he said, as he rested his shaking hand over Jaime's. "And now you both are my friends. You are very generous, my new friend."

Jaime turned. "Let me tell you something. What I do with my money is my business. And what my friend does with the money I've given him is his business. You'd do well to mind your own."

The woman looked at Jaime, shook her head, and walked off to her car. Lisa looked at Jaime, smiled, and then looked back at the woman. "Yeah, you don't even know!" she called out. "She don't even know," Lisa said to herself.

Jaime took Lisa's hand and looked at Bombay. "I hope this helps," he said.

"Thank you, most respected sir."

Jaime narrowed his eyes and looked away. He had become unnerved, and it was obvious. It was as though he'd been found out. "I've got to get my friend to the bus station," he said. Jaime could sense he was in the presence of a seer. Bombay knew. Just like the nuns from his childhood knew.

He held Lisa's hand as they walked back to the car. He grabbed her bags, and they made their way across the street and to the station. At the ticket counter, Lisa pulled on the back of his shirt. "Jaime, are you okay?" She raised up on her toes and spoke softly into his ear. "I don't feel good about leaving you right now."

Jaime closed his eyes. He wanted so badly to ask her to stay, but he couldn't free her from one demon only to place her in the path of another. He turned and brushed Lisa's hair from her face. "I'll be alright Lisa, I promise. Now come on, we need to hurry, or you'll miss your bus." He had to cut the conversation off before it could go any further. He couldn't trust himself. He was in love, and his heart was breaking. Every word threatened to flush the tears and change his mind.

It was noon and time to board. They pushed through the crowd and onto the platform where Lisa handed her bag to the attendant and opened her arms to hug Jaime goodbye. She lifted onto her toes and wrapped her arms around his neck. "I'll miss you, Jaime," she said, and then pulled away before her feelings overwhelmed her, and turned to board the bus. She stopped, grabbed the handle, and leaned out. "I'll write!"

"Do you have my address?"

Lisa stopped and glared right through him. "Jaime!"

Jaime closed his eyes and pressed his fingers into his forehead. "Oh, yeah. That's right."

Lisa was ushered up the steps and down the aisle, where she found and took her seat. As the bus pulled away from the station, she pressed her hand against the window and looking back said, "I love you, Jaime."

It took Jaime a few seconds to realize what he'd read from her lips. He ran after the bus and called back with desperation, "Lisa, don't go!" But it was too late, the bus had turned the corner. Lisa never saw him.

Jaime sat down on the curb, folded his arms across his knees, buried his face, and wept with no sense of his surroundings.

Lisa curled up in her seat, took Jaime's shirt from her bag and buried her face in it, and cried with no sense of her surroundings.

While Lisa and Jaime were crying. Nona was weaving.

CHAPTER 10

I'm Nona, Dear

Jaime lifted his head to the people who were having to go around him on the sidewalk. Through tear-soaked eyes, he returned their curious looks with a glaring dare for any one of them to say something. He pulled his shirttail up, pressed it into his face, and said with a low and failing cry, "Stop looking at me."

His heart was breaking for the second time in his life, only this was somehow different than the day his mother died. That day he felt abandoned. Today he was defeated. As Lisa's bus took her away, whatever thoughts of hope he'd begun to have were now savagely crushed, like the cigarette being ground into the pavement by the boot of the man who was waiting to cross the street in front of him.

For the past two days, Jaime had stood at the gates of heaven. Her eyes, her smile, her singing. Feeling her hold on to him at night, with her face buried into his neck, and knowing they were both safe, was something he'd never known before. Lisa was flooding his world. Maybe life had no meaning, but for those two short days, she had made it worth living.

"Sir..."

"Sir!"

Jaime's trance was broken by a tapping on his shoulder.

"I'm gonna have to ask you to move. You're blocking the sidewalk," the policeman said. "Are you alright? You look distressed."

Jaime stood up. "I'm alright."

He turned his collar, slid his hands into his jacket pockets, and staggered back towards the garage with a revulsion for life that nearly made him physically sick. Turning the corner, Jaime saw Bombay packing his bag and immediately ducked back out. He couldn't handle seeing him right now, so he circled around to the side of the building, lit a cigarette, and waited.

Seeing Bombay reminded Jaime that he needed a job. The money he'd given him, plus the bus ticket, had left him nearly broke. He dropped his head, crushed his cigarette out against the wall, and slung one reluctant foot in front of the other towards the shop to see if the position was still available.

Jaime was being forced to think about the things that had to be done, like getting a job. Lisa was going to have two days on that bus to do nothing but think about Jaime. She pulled a spiral notebook out of her bag and started writing him a letter that she would mail when she reached her sister's house. This way she could tell him about her feelings without the fear of having to watch him explain that he didn't feel the same way about her. Why else would he not have asked her to stay? But Lisa's heart was aching too badly to write. She put her notebook back into her bag and curled up in her seat.

"Excuse me, is anyone sitting here?"

Lisa looked over with her sleepy eyes half-closed to see an older woman standing in the aisle, asking about the empty seat next to her.

"Uh, no."

She watched out of the corner of her eye as the woman sat down and made herself comfortable.

"You go back to sleep dear," she said as she opened her sewing bag. "I've got work to do, and you've been on a long journey."

"It's not been that long," Lisa replied as she closed her eyes.

"I'm not talking about the bus ride, dear. You get some rest now, nous y sommes presque."

Lisa was too tired to ask the woman what she'd meant by that and curled back up with her head resting against the window. She was shaken out of her sleep as the bus stopped to refuel in Memphis and draped across her like a blanket was Jaime's shirt with a heart sewn onto it. She held it up and smiled at the woman. "Thank you. But how did you know?"

"I'm Nona, dear."

Lisa tilted her head and waited for more. When it never came, she held the shirt back up to her cheek. "Well, thank you, Nona."

The bus stopped again near Little Rock, waking Lisa once more as everyone filed through the aisle to get off and find the vending machines and restrooms. She looked over for Nona, but she was gone. Lisa raised up and searched the bus, but she wasn't there. She turned to look out the window when a small boy following his mother down the aisle, leaned in, and stole her attention. "She said to tell you she's not finished."

"What?" Lisa asked.

The boy looked back. "Nona. She's not finished!"

Lisa jumped up out of her seat. "Nona!" she called out. "What? I don't understand. What's going on here? Stop looking at me!" she said to the passengers who were shuffling past her. She collapsed into her seat and looked out her window at the woman who was leading the boy off the bus. She grabbed Jaime's shirt for comfort, and wringing it through her hands, noticed the heart was gone. Lisa stared into the headrest of the seat in front of her. She pushed herself into the aisle and frantically squeezed past the line of passengers to get off the bus and to catch up with the young boy.

"Be careful exiting. I want you to be happy and safe," the bus driver said, as she reached the front.

"I'm sorry, it's just that I've got to, wait, what did you say!"

"I said watch your step ma'am, it's wet outside."

"You said, 'happy and safe'!"

"I think I know what I said, now please, you're holding up the line."

Lisa stepped off the bus in near delirium and looked across the parking lot for the boy. She spotted the woman she assumed was his mother and ran up to her.

"Excuse me, but I need to know what your son meant by that. Can I speak to him? Where is he?"

"I don't know what you're talking about, and I don't have any children. You're mistaking me for someone else, I'm afraid."

"No! I saw him holding your hand as you got off the bus."

"Look, young lady, I told you you're mistaken. Now you're starting to bother me."

"I'm sorry. I just... I just don't understand all of this."

"Well, I'm sorry I can't help you. I hope you find whoever it is you're looking for."

Lisa stood there as the woman walked away. She remembered what Jaime had said to her in the kitchen, and thought to herself, "Now I'm seeing people. And they're all pointing back to that book." She followed the crowd to the restroom where she changed into Jaime's shirt and splashed her face with cold water. She looked up from the sink and into the mirror. "I've gotta find Nona."

Jaime reached for the door just as Bombay was being pushed out by a short, hostile man wearing a vest and a ridiculous looking bow tie.

"You drunks stay out of here! This is your last warning. Next time I'm calling the police!"

Jaime let go of the door, and the irate man went back inside.

"Forgive me, sir," Bombay said, as he brushed past Jaime. He turned, and they made eye contact. "My friend!"

"Bombay! Are you alright?"

"Yes, my friend. But the truth is, and this is the truth, I need something to drink. Just a little something," he said, holding up his hand with thumb and forefinger nearly touching. "This man, he won't let me have any."

"But you have money to buy it, right?"

"Yes, I do. But he won't let me. What can be done though? It's not his fault, he was born with no kindness in his heart."

Jaime set his jaw and glared back into the shop.

"I'll get it for you. What do you want?"

Bombay attempted to hand Jaime the cash he'd given him earlier, but Jaime pushed his hand away.

"A large bottle of mouthwash, please."

"But you can't drink mouthwash. You don't swallow mouthwash; you spit it back out."

Bombay just looked at him.

Jaime looked down at the pavement, and then slightly nodding his head, said under his breath, "Of course."

Bombay shrugged his shoulders.

"Listen, I have to go in here, but I shouldn't be long. Where can I find you?"

"Down this road. Do you see?"

"Yeah..."

"Do you see the church?"

"The church?"

"Yes, the church. Where the dead Jesus lives."

Jaime cut his eyes at Bombay to see if he was meant to laugh at that. He wasn't. He looked back down the road.

"Yeah, I see the church."

"It will be easy for you, my friend. See? It has the same as you."

"What?"

"The cross. Around your neck. See?"

"Oh yeah, I see."

"I'll be waiting for you there. On the bench."

"Okay, I'll try not to be long."

Jaime went in and saw Jasmine being scolded by the red-faced man in the bow tie. The small shop sat underneath the interstate overpass, and the homeless would gather there to find shade from the sun or shelter from the rain. It had bars across the front door and windows, and while the shop had nothing that was really worth breaking in for, those with, just couldn't seem to trust those without. Inside, were three shelves. The center shelf was stocked with dry goods. The shelves on the wall to the right carried basic toiletry items and magazines, and along the wall to the left were the coolers. Straight ahead, in the back of the shop, was the small, enclosed area where the cashier worked. A sliding glass window separated Jasmine from the rest of the shop. And it was there that she was standing with her arms folded, enduring the spit-spewing rage of the small man, who Jaime assumed was the owner. It was too difficult to watch, so Jaime occupied himself by looking over the magazine section and then down the toiletries shelf where he spotted the mouthwash. He moved in closer to see the price when the window slid open.

"Can I help you?" the man asked from the other side of the counter, startling Jaime as though he'd been caught taking the bottle of mouthwash without paying. Which was exactly his intention, just not yet.

"I'm Jaime. I've come to see about the position. Is it still open?"

"Weren't you supposed to be here this morning? I came in because you told Jasmine you'd be here this morning. It's now well past twelve and I've wasted half the day on you."

Jasmine was behind him rolling her eyes and shaking her head.

"Sorry, there was something I had to take care of. But I'm here now. Is the job still available?" Jaime's patience was thinner than his, and he was not in the mood to be polite, but he was having this job.

The man closed the window and came out into the store. He looked Jaime over, looked back at Jasmine who shook her head yes, and then back at Jaime. "Yeah, it's open. I'll pay you a dollar an hour."

"I was told a dollar seventy-five though," Jaime interrupted.

"You want the job or not?"

"Yeah," Jaime said, looking down at him with the same satisfaction as when Raymond was unknowingly challenging Jaime's bottle of water with a bottle of vodka.

"It's part-time. Be here at eight. You'll work till noon, Wednesday through Friday, and noon to six on the weekends. Jasmine can train you, oh, and hand me that application. Here, fill this out and leave it by the register. I'll be back tomorrow to pick it up." He started towards the door and looked back at Jasmine. "Remember what I said!" and then at Jaime, "And you, don't be late!"

Jasmine came out from behind the window. "Don't let him get to you, he only shows up a couple of times a week and all you gotta do is nod your head and pretend you're listening to him."

"So why did he run that guy out of here?" Jaime asked.

"Because he's evil. He hates those folks.'"

"Those folks?"

"Yeah, there's a homeless camp down the road. I let 'em come in. That's what all the shouting was about. He was letting me have it. He knows I do, but I won't admit to it. I mean, if he's not here, he has no way of knowing if I do or not. I feel sorry for them. I wish there was more I could do to help, but at a dollar seventy-five an hour, oh and sorry about that, but he'll give you a raise in six weeks. He just didn't wanna tell you, might make him look nice, you know."

Jaime clenched his fists in his pockets, stiffened his arms, causing his shoulders to rise up his neck, and looked over at the mouthwash.

"You have a troubled soul, don't you?" Jasmine said, but a train rushing by drowned her words.

Jaime looked back, and with a raised voice asked, "Do you know where this camp is?"

"Yeah..."

They were both shouting over the train to one another. She took his arm and led him out the front door.

"You see that church down there?"

"Yeah."

"It's behind it. There's a steep hill that leads down to the river. It's somewhere down there." They both stepped back inside. "Oh! You know that woman that was in here the other day when you came in asking about the job?" The train passed, leaving them shouting, and laughing. "Sorry, these trains though. You remember? Black lady, in her thirties maybe? I think she looks like Cicely Tyson, you know, the actress."

"Yeah, I remember her. Whose paintings are these?"

"They're mine."

Jaime looked closer and then back over at Jasmine. "I quit art school."

"Should've known," she said with a smile.

Jaime narrowed his eyes.

"Not that you quit!" she said with a laugh. "That you're an artist too! You know, same soul in two bodies. We can tell, right?"

"Yeah, I thought so, too," Jaime said, as he moved his eyes into the next painting. "They're passionate."

"Jaime."

"What?"

"Anyway..."

"You probably write too, don't you?"

"I write poetry."

"Can I read it?"

"No!" she said with a laugh.

"Jaime!"

"What!"

"Anyway, she comes in here all the time and just looks around. She's really sweet. Well, she told me where the camp was. She was in the shop one evening and it was storming outside, so I offered to drive her home. She led me to the church and said to let her out, that she could walk from there."

Jaime placed the painting back on the wall and closed his eyes in disbelief that there were people actually living outside. He locked his hands around the back of his neck and closed his elbows in towards his face with a long sigh. "Jasmine, I need to go. I gotta meet someone. So, I'll see you tomorrow?"

"Unless you change your mind."

"No, I'll be here at eight."

Between the moment she'd left the shop and entered her cashier station, Jaime had grabbed the bottle of mouthwash off the shelf and left.

Jasmine mischievously smiled. She'd seen him, and she knew who it was for. "We're gonna get on like a house on fire!" She pulled out the file cabinet drawer and fingered through the receipts for mouthwash, shorting the shop by another bottle. As she had done before.

Jaime's head wilted with a laugh as he walked towards the church, "*where the dead Jesus lives.*"

Lisa closed her eyes and waited for Oklahoma City.

CHAPTER 11

Mary

Bombay wasn't on the bench. Jaime walked around to the back of the church and saw the footpath that led down the hill and towards the river below. As he approached the leafless woods, he could see the colors of the sprawling tarps and tents that were scattered along its banks. Walking into the campsite unannounced didn't seem like a good idea, so he pulled the mouthwash out of his pants, sat down against the graveled edge of the railroad track, lit a cigarette, and thought about what to do when he saw a couple of people walking down the path towards him.

As they approached, he stood up. "Excuse me, but I'm looking for a man called Bombay, do either of you know him? We were supposed to meet up at the church, but he's not there and I wondered if he might be here somewhere."

"Yeah, we know Bombay. If he's here, he's probably over at Monday's. Who are you?"

"I'm Jaime."

"You got another cigarette?"

"Yeah." Jaime opened his pack and they both helped themselves.

"Thanks, they call me Rookie."

"And I'm Carol. I see you brought Bombay his favorite drink," she said with a laugh.

"Yeah. That's why I'm looking for him."

"I guess Cyril must've been in the shop," Rookie said, shaking his head.

"Cyril?"

"Yeah, the guy that owns the shop up the road. I recognized the bottle. That's that nasty mouthwash he sells. I figured Bombay must've asked you to go in and get it for him. Cyril won't let us come in there."

"Oh, him. Yeah, he was there."

"The girl's really nice," Carol said. "She lets us..."

"Jasmine."

"Yeah, Jasmine's her name, and well, she lets us come in. But if Cyril's there..."

"Yeah, if Cyril's there..." Rookie made a kicking motion with his leg.

Jaime drew long on his cigarette and looked up the hill towards the church. "Well, I start work there in the morning." He turned his head back and looked at the both of them. "And y'all can come in whenever you want, whether you have money or not."

"What do you mean, 'money or not'?" Carol asked.

"I mean, Cyril has no idea how generous he's about to become." Jaime took the last drag from his cigarette. "Could we see if Bombay's around?"

Carol and Rookie looked at each other. "Come on, Jaime," Carol said, as she brushed the hood back from her head.

Jaime followed.

The scene was hard for him to take in. "These people are so tired, so cold, so worn down, so hopeless. They move like shadows across a post-apocalyptic landscape. The river that runs next to them is high and provides the soundtrack to their lives. There's garbage everywhere, but what can they do? And why would they even care anymore? But of course like everyone else, they do." Jaime thought to himself as he made his way through, and closer to the fire pit. "So this is what it looks like beyond the margins of our pretty pages." As much as this angered him, he could sense a grounding. He felt that he was among people and not actors. He followed Carol and Rookie to the circle gathered around the fire, when...

"My friend!"

Jaime looked over to see Bombay rising up and walking towards him, arms opened for an embrace.

"I'm sorry I missed you. The holy man from the church said I had to leave the bench. I was out of compliance."

Jaime raked his hands down his face, pulling his cheeks from his eyes. Pausing, with his fingertips at his jawline, he stared into the void. Churches made him want to kill himself. They were dens of thieves and wolves masquerading as saints and lambs. And they ruled the world. He collected himself, and turned,

"You weren't in compliance with what?" he asked. Bombay stood silent, his arms still open. Jaime gave up and stepped into his embrace. As he turned his head to settle onto Bombay's shoulder, he saw Mary. He reached out and presented the bottle of mouthwash to Bombay.

"As promised, my friend."

Bombay took the bottle and returned to his place next to Monday.

"You are most trusted," he said, as he twisted the top. "Please sit with us."

Jaime approached the fire ring and walked towards her. "Mary?" he asked.

Mary turned and looked up at him, and then moved down the log that was being used like a church pew. "I remember you," she said. "You helped me yesterday, outside the shop up on the hill."

Jaime sat down beside her. "Yeah, I'm sorry I didn't make it back this morning."

"It's okay, dear. I didn't make it either. What in the world are you doing here?"

"Well, I came down to see if I could find Bombay, and I met Carol and Rookie. I'm glad I found you."

"I'm glad you did too, dear. You're a real blessing." Mary looked at the curious faces sitting around the fire. "Hey everyone, this is my new friend..."

"Jaime."

"Yes," she laughed while placing her lilting but reassuring hand on his shoulder, "Jaime." Beginning from her right, she made the introductions: "These two inseparable ones are Briena and Monday, Bombay, you already know him, Marti, and you already know Rookie and Carol too, that's Joey, and Aimee and Imani, who was sitting next to him completing the circle. Dito's not here, and there are others, but you'll meet them soon enough."

Rookie looked around at the uncertain and uninterested faces and said, "He's gonna start working at the shop on the hill tomorrow."

Still no interest, until…

"And he said we don't need no money to shop there!" Carol added.

Everyone's attention was now lit as they cut their eyes at Jaime, waiting to hear more. Jaime cut his eyes over at Carol, wishing she'd said less.

"Really?" Imani asked.

"Of course you need money, Carol, if you're gonna *buy* something," Jaime said, as he was looking into the flame of his lighter.

The campsite went silent. Everyone was trying to collectively confirm what they all understood him to be saying by covert eye contact. And of course, it's best to keep quiet and go with what you think, when what you think is better than what might actually be true. So, without a word spoken, everyone understood that no one was to ask for clarification, just go with it. Except Monday.

"So, you mean we can take whatever we want?"

"Monday!" everyone shouted. Briena put her hand over his mouth.

Imani scolded him. "What the hell's that matter with you?"

"Sorry, I just thought…"

Jaime sensed it all and changed the subject to lighten the mood and rescue him from being the center of attention. "Hey, hey, hey." He turned towards Mary. "Hey Mary, you know what?"

"What?" Mary asked, still looking sour-faced at Monday.

"You look like Cicely Tyson!"

Everyone around the circle laughed and turned to each other with, "She does."

Monday interrupted with, "Well, I think she looks like..."

Mary stopped him short. "Watch it Monday! You know you look like a third-stage werewolf!"

Everyone laughed out loud. Monday spewed his drink with an explosion of laughter and shrugged his shoulders. "What can I say, she's right."

"Hey, Jaime!" Imani said, pushing her elbow into his side, "You know, you look like Eric Clapton."

Jaime rolled his eyes. "Jesus though, "*Tales of Brave Ulysses*," I wish I could play guitar like that."

"Well Imani," Jaime pushed his elbow in return, "you know when I first saw you, I thought you looked a lot like Lyndon Johnson." Intentionally trolling for a laugh and hoping for the results he got.

"Oh, you done messed up boy!" Imani said, laughing with her arms outstretched to strangle him. She pushed him onto his back, both laughing. "Wait!" Jaime said, raising up on his elbows, "I meant Dianna Ross!"

"That's better!" she said, brushing her hair back, holding an imaginary microphone and over-dramatically launching into, "*Ain't no mountain high enough, ain't no valley low enough...*"

Aimee jumped up and took the imaginary microphone from Imani and finished, *"To keep me from you."* Everyone laughed and applauded, except Jaime. He thought of Lisa, leaned over towards Joey, and asked, "Could I have a drink of that? I'll pay you back."

"There's more where this came from. Help yourself. And there ain't no paying back 'round here."

Joey handed him the bottle of vodka, and he turned it up like water. While everyone else spent the next hour sorting out what famous personality each of them did or didn't look like, breaking out in either laughter or near fighting, Jaime thought of Lisa.

Imani finally reached over and politely took the bottle from him.

"Sorry," he said.

"It's okay, love, but you need to slow down, you're drunk. Can I just set this over here? We don't wanna have to carry you back up that hill."

"Yeah."

Bombay was watching closely. "My friend, the girl who was with you in the garage, how is she?"

Ezra sat down beside Jaime. "Yes, how *is* Lisa, my friend?"

Jaime recognized the voice, and turned." What are you doing here?"

Ezra reached into the fire and pulled a coal out. He turned it in his hand and studied it with some curiosity.

"What are you doing here!" Jaime shouted

"You know," Ezra said as he tossed the coal over his shoulder.

"Yeah, I know. And I know what you're trying to do. You want me to kill myself, just like you did. It's because of you that she's not here! And if she were, I wouldn't even be talking to you."

Everyone looked at Jaime and then around the circle at each other, wide-eyed and speechless.

"I told you, love is nothing more than a useless drug. The one thing you thought might have made life worth living is gone. I'm sure someone around here has a razor, ask 'em."

Jaime stood up. "Look, I'm sorry about what happened between you and Celia, but Lisa said she loves me. I saw her say it. She told me she'd write me, and when she does, I'm gonna write her back and ask her to come home."

"Fool! She's never gonna write you."

Jaime leaned forward and put his finger in the face of someone who wasn't there. "You leave her alone! I don't care about myself, but I swear to god, if you…"

"Jaime! Is everything okay?" asked Briena.

"Yeah, I gotta go." Jaime turned and staggered out of the camp.

A light rain began to fall. Everyone started leaving the circle and making their way to their tents for the night, except Bombay. He wrapped himself in a blanket and went to look for Jaime. He climbed the hill and searched for him as he made the long walk back to the garage. He didn't find him, but he noticed Jaime's car was still parked where he'd left it that morning. Bombay curled up in his usual corner. "Don't let them take you tonight, my friend," he said as he closed his eyes.

Jaime had wandered off the path and was lying unconscious, face down on the hill outside the camp, while Lisa's bus was pulling into the Oklahoma City station. It was one o'clock in the morning and Lisa was sound asleep. Everyone had exited the bus except her. The driver walked back and gently tapped her on the shoulder. "Miss... you need to wake up. We're here."

Lisa turned her head, grabbed her backpack, and stumbled half-awake down the aisle and off the bus. The driver reached underneath the carriage and pulled her bag out. It was heavy, but Lisa dragged it towards the ticket counter, with her backpack hanging from her shoulder.

"Excuse me, I have a connection to Albuquerque that is scheduled to leave at ten. Is it running on time?"

"Yes ma'am, it is."

"Okay, thank you. Do you know if there's a public library near here?"

"There's one about a mile down that road sweetie, Reno Avenue. It opens at nine."

"Oh, okay. Thank you."

Lisa walked over to the waiting area, laid across two seats with her backpack as a pillow, and went to sleep.

Like blinds slowly lifting, Lisa's eyes opened to the morning light that was streaming through the station. Her body had stiffened on the hard-plastic chairs, but she managed to raise up and look over at the terminal clock. Lisa didn't like to swear, but "Goddammit!" she cried out loud. It was almost nine. The woman a few seats over covered her daughter's ears with her hands. Lisa looked over and apologized before brushing her hair out of her face and trying to collect her thoughts. She didn't have much time, as she was going to be on foot, so she started going through her larger bag looking for anything that she absolutely wanted to keep. She was going to have to ditch it and go with only the one she could carry on her shoulder. As she made room in her backpack, she found the money that Jaime had tucked inside. Her heart sank. She packed everything that she could fit into her backpack, ditched the large one, and was now able to hail a cab.

Lisa thumbed through the handful of dollars, paid the driver, and rushed inside.

"Can you point me to your reference section?"

The young man behind the counter put his finger to his lips and shushed her. "Please ma'am, keep your voice down. This is a library. And yes," he pointed with his shushing finger, "just over there against the far wall."

"Sorry, and thank you," she whispered.

Lisa hurriedly walked over and started looking up and down the shelves. "F,F,F, there it is!" She pulled the book off the shelf, sat down at the table, and started digging through it until she found the entry.

"The Fate, in Greek and Roman mythology, refers to any of the three goddesses who spun the threads of human destiny. The Fates were personified as three very old sisters whose names were Clotho (Spinner), Lachesis (Allotter), and Atropos (Inflexible). Clotho spun the "thread" of human fate, the Romans identified her as Nona...

Lisa froze.

"Nona."

She slowly closed the book, scooted her chair back, and walked over to the window. With a faraway stare, Lisa thought back to the book her sister used to read to her, and all that had taken place on the bus. She took a deep breath. "I have to go back." Making the connection to Albuquerque was no longer her concern. She needed a ticket back to Jaime. But he hadn't left her enough money for that. She'd have to find a way to come up with it. Before placing the book back on the shelf, Lisa turned back to the entry and carefully and quietly tore the page out. The boy, the heart, Nona, the bus driver's words, had all disappeared, but this page was staying with her. She folded it and slid it into the back pocket of her jeans, slung her backpack over her shoulder, and walked out of the library as Carol and Rookie were walking into the shop.

"Is Jaime here?" Rookie asked.

"No, he was supposed to be here an hour ago."

"We're worried about him. Can you help us find him?"

Jasmine turned the sign on the door from open to closed and followed them out, while the police pulled Raymond's body from the river.

CHAPTER 12

I Hope You're Right

There wasn't much that Lisa hated more than a mission. It wasn't the people who stayed there, but the people who ran them. She had spent the night in a holding cell a few years back, picked up after the city's curfew while walking home from a friend's house. That wasn't uncommon for young, brown teens in El Paso. And just like jail, in a mission you were treated harshly for who you were perceived to intrinsically be, not for anything you'd done. But at least in jail, you weren't subjected to this treatment by a staff pretending to be Christian. Lisa's only experience in a mission was in the town she'd just left. Hers was a relatively short stay, but she remembered those she'd seen who had to stay longer, or even indefinitely, and had always felt sorry for them.

They would come in tired, hungry, cold, or hot, scared, and hopeless. Hopeless. That was the thing. There didn't seem to be an end in sight. And the one place they should have been welcomed and treated with sympathy and compassion, they were

THE DISHWASHER — 113

instead typically treated as a nuisance by a short-tempered, con-descending staff. And all in the name of Jesus.

Lisa looked up and down the streets of a city she knew noth-ing about, thought for a moment, and went back into the library and up to the front desk.

"Excuse me, but would you know where I can find a job? I'm trying to earn enough money for a bus ticket."

The head librarian, who was sorting through mail, overheard Lisa and walked over to her.

"Did you say you're looking for work?"

"Yes, ma'am."

The young man at the counter looked up and back over his shoulder. "We could use someone to change out the cards in the children's section, I doubt I'm ever gonna get that done."

"That's what I was thinking, Simon. What's your name?"

"I'm Lisa, Lisa Harris.

"Well Lisa, I'll pay you fifty dollars to go through all the books in the children's section and replace the full check-out cards with new ones. It'll probably take you a few days though. Can you do that? And do you think that'll be enough for a ticket?"

"Yes, I can do that, and I think it will be. Thank you so much!"

"Okay, be here tomorrow morning at nine and ask for me, Mrs. Conner, and we'll get you started."

"I'll be here! And thank you again."

Her excitement was immediately tempered as the front door closed behind her, and she thought about what the night held ahead of her. She crossed the street and asked a man lying on a bench if he could give her directions to the local mission.

He sat up. "Follow this street until you see Reno Avenue and then turn right. It'll be about four blocks down. You won't get in now though. They don't start signing us in until five."

"Okay, thank you," Lisa replied. "And I didn't mean to imply that you..."

"It's alright dear, there's no shame in being homeless, and yeah, I look the part, don't I?" he said with a laugh. "Oh, and don't have alcohol on your breath or you won't get in at all."

"I won't," Lisa said, as she started counting what money she had left. She'd have to make it stretch, but she was hungry, so she started walking in the direction of the mission, looking for a place to eat.

"So, what's got y'all worried," Jasmine asked as she locked up the shop.

Carol picked up what was left of a cigarette from the sidewalk. "He left the campsite late last night and Bombay said this morning..."

"Wait, he was at the campsite?"

Rookie scanned the sidewalk for another cigarette. "Yeah, and Bombay left a little while after him and said he couldn't find him, and that his car was still in the garage."

Carol stopped and lit her half-smoked cigarette. "And he said he was starting work this morning at the shop, so we came here looking for him."

"We were kinda worried. Before he left last night, he was talking to somebody sitting beside him, but there wasn't nobody sitting beside him," Rookie said.

"Isn't that him?" Jasmine asked as they approached the church.

"Where?"

"There, on the bench."

"Yeah, that's him!"

"Jaime!" Carol called out. "Are you okay? Where'd you go last night?"

Jaime lifted his head. He was writing something on a crumpled-up piece of paper. "I slept back there, on the hill."

They all looked at one another, waiting for someone to say something, anything. Carol finally broke the silence and turned towards Jaime. "Looks like you need a bath."

Jasmine looked away and covered her face to hide her laughter. "Well, he does," Carol said. "Look at him. And his hair's all messed up."

"I was on my way to work and..."

Jasmine cut him off. "Well, get up off that bench then, and let's go. You don't wanna be fired before your first day even starts!"

Jaime stood up, braced, and steadied himself with the help of Jasmine's shoulder. "Alright."

A block away from the shop, Jasmine stopped and stretched her arms out. "Shit! Y'all, hold up. I just saw Cyril. We gotta hurry and get in there! Carol, you and Rookie can't come in right now, but I'll come out and get you as soon as he leaves. And I'll put some coffee on."

"Okay, thanks," Rookie said.

"Come on Jaime, we gotta get inside before he does!"

Jasmine and Jaime didn't have time to get behind the counter. She had just flipped the sign back to *We're Open* when they heard him unlocking the back door. Jasmine grabbed Jaime and pulled him over to the magazine rack and pretended to be showing him around the shop, just as Cyril came walking through.

"Jasmine! Make sure the trash gets out. The collection will be here in about an hour. And break those boxes down that are stacked out back and get them in the dumpster too. I gotta go, I just came by to..." Cyril looked over at Jaime, squinted his eyes, looked him up and down, and shook his head. "This will not do. You look like you slept outside!" He turned to Jasmine with a look that said, "Get this cleaned up, or else." She nodded her head. "Anyway," he continued, "I came by to pick up the forms I left for you to fill out. Where are they?"

Jaime reached into his back pocket and presented Cyril with the forms he had completed while recovering on the bench in front of the church. "Here they are."

Cyril took them, turned once more back to Jasmine, locked his eyes on hers, and mouthed the words, "You told me to hire him!"

The front doorbells rang as a woman entered the shop.

"We got everything under control Cyril. Now you go do what you gotta do," Jasmine said while ushering him out the back.

"Excuse me, do you all sell stockings?"

Jaime nearly fell, as he missed the step down from the back of the shop.

He came closer and the woman leaned in towards him and whispered, "I'm glad they let y'all come in. I know there's lots of places around here that won't."

"I work here," Jaime said.

Jasmine had just returned from escorting Cyril out and wilted with laughter at the expression on the woman's face.

Jaime side-eyed her.

"Oh no! You put those eyes right back straight! You did this to yourself!"

The woman looked confused. "So you do sell, um... Well, I'll just get those stockings and be on my way."

With Cyril gone, Jasmine went out to let Carol and Rookie in for coffee. By then, Mary had joined them. As they all came in, Jaime tried to look away, but Mary's presence was too strong. "Can I take this one outside for a bit?" Mary asked Jasmine, as she grabbed Jaime's arm.

"Of course. Just don't let him escape. At some point, he has to actually help me in here!"

Mary brought Jaime outside and sat him down on an up-turned bucket. She pulled one up beside him. But before she could get a word out, Jaime launched into a tirade.

"Mary, how can you possibly believe that there's a god who's watching out for you? I'm sorry, but you're fucking living in the woods! This makes me so angry. Is he powerless, or careless?"

Mary smiled and took Jaime's hand. "He's neither, dear boy. Don't be so angry. Don't you know he's got a beautiful place set aside for me soon? I've put all my faith in him, and he's just getting it ready."

Jaime stood up and started pacing. "But Mary…"

"Settle down, boy. You're restless. Settle down." She tapped on the bucket. "Sit."

Jaime sat back down but was rocking back and forth with pent-up appeals to this god of hers. "How can she be so at peace with this?" he thought to himself. "Why doesn't this god act now?" He pulled the bottle of vodka out from the inner pocket of his jacket. It was still half-full. He drank half and looked over at Mary, who asked for the rest.

Jaime handed her the bottle. "I love you, Mary."

"I love you more, sweet boy," she said, "and I'm praying for you." Mary downed the last of the vodka and stood up. "I got no money, dear, but I need some things."

Jaime stood up too. "Come on inside. Get whatever you need, Mary."

"See? He's watching out for me," she said, as she reached over to hug him.

Jaime wrapped her up tight in his arms and bit his tongue. And then bit it again and again. And then finally said under his breath, "I hope you're right."

The day had ended, and Jaime pulled up to see two policemen at Lisa's door. He'd been expecting this day to come, and for an instant, he thought of giving in. He continued on to the back of the house, pulled a bottle of vodka out from under his seat, and grabbed the shirt that was lying on the passenger side floor. With his eyes locked into the rearview mirror, he emptied the bottle onto the shirt, and hurriedly tried to wipe down as much as he could of the passenger side seat, door, window, and dashboard. He got out of the car, wadded the shirt up around the bottle, and pushed it down into the trashcan on his way towards the front of the house. He confronted them both as they were just rounding the corner.

"Mr. Felts?"

"Uh yeah, I'm Mist…, uh yeah, I'm him," Jaime stuttered out.

"Can you tell us anything about your neighbor, Raymond Gillis?"

"What do you want to know?"

"His body was found in the river, south of town. Would you know anything about that?"

"No."

"He lived with a Miss Lisa Harris. Would you have any idea where we might find her? We've knocked but there's no answer."

Jaime went silent.

They walked around to the back of the house. "Is this your car?"

"Yeah."

The two officers looked at one another and grinned.

Raymond's body had been found with the cable still tied to him, and it didn't take much work to find the tire at the bottom of the pool, the only place deep enough in that section to have submerged him. Finding the vehicle to match the tire however was going to take a lot of work, or at least that's what the police had thought. Until Jaime pulled up.

"Would you mind opening the hood? We wanna look at your spare tire."

"I don't have a spare tire."

"You don't? Open it anyway."

"Have you been drinking, Mr. Felts?" The one asked as he looked over and into the hood.

"No, you can give me a sobriety test if you want."

They looked at one another and then back at Jaime.

"That won't be necessary, but we're gonna need you to come down to the station with us for questioning."

Jaime looked over his glasses and across the table. "I told you, I fell asleep. I never noticed that he hadn't come back with the gasket till the next morning. Can I have another cigarette?"

"No, you've had five already. You nervous?"

"No, I'm bored."

Chief Dodson got up from the table and motioned with her head for Captain Thomas to follow her outside the interrogation room."

"You got nothing on him, Don."

"I know he did it."

"We've been through this a thousand times. I appreciate your instincts, but you don't know that he did it, and even if you did, it doesn't matter. You can't prove it."

Captain Thomas huffed and slammed his fist on the wall.

"It's odd, though. I mean he looks like he doesn't even care," Chief Dodson said, looking at Jaime through the window.

"Exactly! That's the kinda person who could do something like this. This wasn't done on impulse. It took a cold calculated nerve."

"You're just furious 'cause this kid's not afraid of you. Don't make it personal. Let him go, Don. At least until you actually have something on him."

Captain Thomas swung the door open, "You're free to go, but don't even think about leaving town. We're not finished."

Jaime looked over at him and suppressed his laughter. His expression reminded Jaime of John when he sulked off to wash dishes at the restaurant.

Jaime's heart hurt as he stepped into the kitchen where Lisa had last made him breakfast. He wondered where she was, and if she missed him. Without her, his will to go on was weakening.

Lisa stood in line at the mission for dinner. Believing now, that it was her fate to be with Jaime, her will to get back was strengthening.

CHAPTER 13

What About Now

Jaime pressed his back against the door, slowly closing it behind him. He turned on the lamp in the kitchen and reached for a bottle from the cupboard above the sink. The thing about feeling alone is that you can be in the middle of a sidewalk with people all around you, or at the campsite-talking and laughing, and still know that you're alone. But remove the distractions, and step into that empty house, where she once was, and your soul becomes just as empty. It's as though nothing else exists, or ever has, but your broken heart.

He sat down at the table, lit a cigarette, leaned back, and looked over at the bed, where the sheets lay open from the night before, and thought about Albuquerque. "They'd know if I left town," he thought to himself. "But even if they did, how would they ever find me in New Mexico?" He got up and started pacing the floor. "Look, the only thing they got is that spare tire, and how are they ever gonna connect that to you?" Jaime was now talking to himself out loud. He took a drink and massaged his forehead. "There's no way they have anything else." But his mind went back to Captain Thomas' words. "We're not finished."

He walked over to the refrigerator, opened the door, and looked around before closing it. "They're thinking, they're working, they're not letting this go. I mean really, how many people actually get away with murder?" he asked himself. "What if they figure it out?" The vodka was firing his imagination. "I gotta get outta here." He started rearranging the things on the table: the salt and pepper shakers, the vinegar bottle, his keys. "At least Lisa's safe," he thought.

During the questioning, Jaime told the police he had bought Lisa a bus ticket out of town, but he lied about where, because he was afraid of them suspecting her and trying to track her down. He grabbed the bottle, tilted it, and examined the Russian label. "They think she's in Oklahoma City, but by now she's safe and with her sister in Albuquerque."

Lisa took her tray and gave it to the woman behind the window. She followed the others downstairs and towards the chapel for the mandatory evening prayer service. Two police officers were standing at the check-in desk. As she walked past them, she overheard one of them asking about a Lisa Harris. She gasped. Her heart was pounding. She had no idea what they could be talking about, but she was a Native American woman, staying in a homeless shelter in a Southwestern city, being asked about by two white male cops to a white male attendant. "This was never gonna be alright," she thought.

She tried to control her panic and said to the person next to her, "I, uh, I gotta go back and get my..." She was scared to death. "My bible. I forgot my bible." She turned and hurried against the flow of those streaming into the chapel. "I gotta get outta here," she thought as she made her way back to the women's dorm. She grabbed her bag and rejoined the stream. Watching the front desk attendant out of the corner of her eye, she waited. When he looked down at his records, she made her move, squeezed herself out of line, and ran.

Jaime walked over and opened the cabinets above the kitchen counter, and started looking at the cereal boxes, wondering why he had cereal. "You would never find her though," he said to himself. "You don't know her sister's name, and even if you did..." Jaime stopped, put the cereal box back in the cabinet, and remembered Lisa as she boarded the bus. "She said she'd write." He closed the cabinet door and braced his arms stiff against the sink. "If she writes, I'll have the return address." He walked over and straightened the blanket that was covering the kitchen window. "You're just gonna have to wait and see if she writes." He moved the blanket and looked outside. Everything was dark and still. He walked back to the table and took a long drink. "And if she doesn't, well, it doesn't matter then does it?"

Lisa turned the corner and stopped to catch her breath. Scared and confused, she looked around to see if anyone was following her. The streets were empty. She walked up the road that would lead her back to the library. She turned and saw lights coming up behind her, ran and ducked into a parking garage. She stood still against the wall as the police car slowly entered. As it turned towards the second floor, Lisa frantically started trying the car doors until she finally found one unlocked. She crawled into the backseat and stared up at the ceiling. She could only imagine that this had something to do with Raymond, but what? Maybe that was it though. Maybe he'd gotten himself into trouble again and was sitting in jail. Maybe that's where he'd been the last few days. But why would the police be looking for her? She grabbed Jaime's shirt and pulled it up to her face. "I want him out of my life." She slowly pulled the shirt back down. "And what if he *is* in jail? That means at some point he'll be getting out. How can I go back to Jaime if he's gonna be there?"

Just then she heard a couple of car doors closing. She raised up and peeked out the window and saw the police officers shining flashlights in the cars that were parked down at the end of the row. Lisa quietly opened the door and snuck out. She crawled along the side of the car and crossed over to the far end of the garage, hiding behind one car to the next, until she reached the pedestrian door. She looked back and waited, making sure she wasn't in their view, and ran out. She crossed the street and hid in the bushes against the library.

Moving away from a fire and into a cold tent is a ruthless way to treat those you've designed and created, but Mary trusted this god, and so she crossed herself, looked over her shoulder at that dark and dismal triangle, passed on her turn at the bottle, and announced her move to the flickering faces gathered in close around the fire. "Goodnight y'all, I'm gonna turn in."

"Goodnight, Mary," they all replied.

"Y'all don't stay up too late," she said with a weary smile, as she slowly stood up and gathered in the blanket draped around her shoulders.

Mary was full of grace, and for her to be crawling into the hole of a tent to find warmth and rest was a cold-blooded insult to her dignity. She had come to this area on account of the persecutions from the whites in the Deep South. Mary had considered leaving so many times before, but one night she had a dream. An angel had announced that the governor was coming for her, and she was to escape by running north and into the mountains. She woke up in the middle of the night, covered in sweat and fearing for her life. Mary believed in dreams, so the following morning, she packed what she could in a small suitcase, and drove her mule of a car until it broke down on the outskirts of this town in the Appalachian foothills. She took comfort in believing that she had reached this place by divine protection, but she had no money for a room in the local inns, and she was left with no choice but to take shelter where she could. On her first night, three men from the east side of town came in bringing gifts. "We heard that you were here, so we brought you blankets, food, and clothes."

"Thank you all, but how did you find me?" Mary asked.

"The light," they said. "When we parked up on the hill, our headlights shone down upon your tent. We left them on and followed the light to you. We were taking these to the mission when we saw Joseph outside. He told us about you, and that you had just come to town and had nothing and nowhere to go, and that he'd given you this tent. He said he'd shown you the way to this campsite, and that the folks here were kind and generous, and they would take you in."

Mary received their gifts, closed her eyes in thankful humility to god, and asked them to pray for her.

"Blessed are you Mary..." one of the three began, but Mary was already falling asleep. They stopped, covered her in blankets, crossed their hearts over her, and returned to their car.

Jaime crawled into bed and pulled the pillow against him; the one Lisa had used. He could smell her hair. He rolled over onto his side and stared through the darkness and into the wall that separated his side of the house from hers. He remembered the sounds of her suffering, and then remembered the sounds of her singing. Restless, he reached over to the bedside table and grabbed a cigarette. Propping his pillow up against the wall, and still holding on to Lisa's, he started to think of everything. And he thought of Mary.

"How can she believe this?" he thought. "I mean..." His mind started scrolling back to all he had ever known about the Christian faith, and he could find nothing that would vindicate her trust. "I don't understand. Is there no power, nor will from this god to protect her? Why does she wait on him? Is it all about gritting your teeth and holding out hope that you've adhered to the right formula that will reward you with some disembodied afterlife? What about now?" It all came down to power and will. "Does this god not have the power? Or does he just not have the will?" Jaime crushed his cigarette out in the dish on the table beside him and decided to put the power and the will of this god to a test. He removed the cross from around his neck and placed it on the bedside table.

"My mother believed in you, too," he said. "I don't. So, if you're out there, prove me wrong."

Jaime looked up at the missing tile in the ceiling, dismissed his second thoughts, rolled over onto Lisa's side of the bed, and closed his eyes.

Mary had learned that blankets were worth as much underneath you as they were on top. She laid them out onto the cold hard ground, and then curled up with one wrapped around her, and began her nightly prayers.

"Dear Lord, thank you for letting me see another day. Thank you for protecting me and giving me a warm place to sleep. And thank you for my new friend, Jaime. Please watch over him tonight, Lord. Ease his angry heart and protect him from evil..." The wind ruffled the sides of the tent. Mary opened her eyes, "Forgive us our sins Father," and then drew the blanket over her face.

The wind blew the blanket through the cracks in the bedroom window, waking Jaime. He opened his eyes to the beaked man from his childhood sitting above him. His hand was searching through Jaime's chest like an eel. Ezra was also sitting above him, holding his arms out. With no physical resistance however, Jaime reached over to the bedside table and grabbed the cross. As he placed it around his neck, Ezra and the demon skulked away. Ezra to his place in the ceiling, and the beaked man through the wall separating Jaime's room from the space next door, where Raymond had practiced his evil. Jaime fell back asleep, comforted in knowing that he was tangled up in a world that was just as mad as he thought it was.

The wind blew across the banners that hung from the library above her. "Where are you now, Nona?" Lisa asked, as she hid under the bushes. The sound of someone walking up startled her.

"Here young lady," the old man said, as he handed her a blanket.

"You're the man who gave me directions to the mission."

"I saw you from my bench over there. Were you not able to get in?"

"Uh... no, I was too late."

"Well, that blanket should keep you warm tonight."

"Thank you, sir," Lisa said as she wrapped herself up. "I can return it to you in the morning."

"Just give it to Nona, I'm sure she'll see you before I will."

"What?"

"I said I'll be over there on the bench, but there's no hurry to give it back. Keep it for as long as you need it."

Lisa turned her head and stared into the night sky. Blinking back her tears, she curled up and pulled the blanket over her head. "Thank you," she said from underneath it.

CHAPTER 14

Let's Get You Back to Him

Lisa had never slept outside before and being awakened by the sound of traffic made her feel as though her vulnerability was being announced to the world. She pulled the blanket down from over her head, clutched it tightly around her face and just below her squinting eyes that were trying to adjust to the morning light. Cold and stiff, she longed for a hot bath. She had no idea what time it was, but she didn't want to be late for her job at the library.

Even in the worst of times, and there had been too many, Lisa had never given up hope. She could always set her heart on new horizons, and that is a gift that had probably kept her alive. She was nervous about the days ahead, but she trusted that they held her way back to Jaime. She rubbed the heels of her hands into her eyes, and then ran her fingers through her long black hair. She watched for a break in the traffic at the intersection, and then came out of the bushes. She looked over at the bench across the street for her one friend, but he wasn't there. She was tired and disoriented, as people were pushing past her to get into the church that was just a block down from the library.

She scanned the moving world around her. Everyone was dressed in their Sunday best. There was nothing she could do to improve her appearance, so she gathered herself together mentally, set the blanket down on the bench across the way, and walked into the library.

"Good Morning, Lisa!" Mrs. Conner said from across the counter.

"I'm sorry, I know I'm late." Lisa had forgotten the librarian's name. "I promise I'll do a good job though," she said. "Please let me do this. Please?"

"You're not late, but..." Mrs. Conner hesitated, "are you okay dear?"

The front door swung open, and two police officers entered and walked up to the counter. Lisa instinctively moved away from them.

Mrs. Conner looked at them and sighed.

"We're looking for a Lisa Harris, mid-twenties, Indian..."

"Do you mean Native American?" Mrs. Conner interjected. "Or is she from India?"

"Well, yes," the officer replied. "She's an Indian."

"Is she American?"

They both looked at each other and then back at Mrs. Conner.

"She's from Santa Fe," one of them said, "She's an..."

"That's not an Indian!" Mrs. Conner replied, preparing them for a lecture. She looked across the library at Lisa, and with a slight tilt of her head, motioned for her to hide.

Lisa was terrified. She stepped behind one of the bookshelves and listened in on the conversation, keeping one eye on the back door, in case she needed to run.

Mrs. Conner searched for patience from on high. "So, you mean she's American, right?"

Before he could answer, she continued, "We have her name. Thank you, and I'll let you know if we come across her, but we haven't."

"She may be homeless," the officer said, "and we know those people camp out in here."

Mrs. Conner looked at him with disgust but managed to gather herself and reply without spitting anger in his face. "Yeah, they do, and we welcome them. As I've said, we have her name. Good day officer..."

"Callahan."

"Good day, Officer Callahan."

The police officers looked at one another, each hoping the other would say something to break the awkwardness of being on this unfamiliar end of intimidation, but no words came.

Mrs. Conner waited. "Good day, officers," she said with a tone that assured them she was finished.

"Be sure to contact us if you see her, she could be dangerous."

Mrs. Conner exchanged one last glancing look at them as they left the library, before walking over to Lisa who was sitting, head in hands, in the children's section. She pulled up a child sized chair next to hers and asked, "Do you wanna talk about this Lisa?"

"I'm not in trouble, Mrs. Conner. I haven't done anything wrong. I promise. I don't know why they're looking for me. I left Tennessee on Thursday, to go and stay with my sister in Albuquerque. The man I was living with disappeared a few days ago, and he was always in trouble with the law. I just think it has something to do with him."

"But why are you here in Oklahoma City?"

Lisa looked away. "You'll think it's silly."

"Try me," Mrs. Conner said.

"There's this guy..."

"Oh, Lisa..."

"He lives on the other side of our duplex. When Raymond disappeared, he took me in and made me feel safe. I didn't love Raymond, but I fell in love with Jaime."

"Who is Raymond?"

"The guy I was living with; the one I told you about. I met him when I first got to town there. I was staying in the mission and was scared. He was a guy that none of the other guys would mess with, so I pretended to like him, so he'd protect me. When he finally got a place to rent, he talked me into coming with him."

"And he disappeared?"

"Yeah, one night he never came back. Have you ever felt the sense of both anxiety and relief all at once?"

"No, I haven't, but I'm listening, sweetie."

"I went next door to check on him. He had gone to help Jaime, my neighbor, with his plumbing, but he never came back."

"Lisa."

"It's okay. He would hit me a lot, and then he'd make me do things, and hit me even harder if I tried not to. Have you ever felt that?"

Mrs. Conner closed her eyes. "No, I haven't." She gathered herself and took Lisa's hands in hers.

"You wanna talk about Jaime?"

"Yeah."

"Tell it to me slowly."

"He's warm and safe and caring. I love him, but I don't know if he loves me back."

"Did he do or say anything that would make you think he might?"

"He let me stay with him the last two nights, no sex, just holding each other. We both seemed to need holding. Anyway, when he held me like that, I thought maybe he loved me, but I was too afraid to ask. And then he bought me a bus ticket, and I kept hoping he'd ask me not to go, but he didn't."

"Did you ever think he might be feeling the same, but was afraid to say anything? Just like you?"

Lisa closed her eyes and hung her head, "No."

"Lisa, I've talked with you for what, twenty minutes now? You're so lovable. What is it that makes you wonder?"

"I've never been in love, until now, and I'm just afraid of him not loving me back. I don't know."

"And he never tried anything?"

"No. He offered to sleep on the sofa, but I asked him to sleep with me 'cause I was scared."

"I think he loves you, sweetie. Let me ask you, when you two were lying together, did he ever reach over and brush your hair back from your face?"

"Yes. And it felt so nice when he did that."

"Let's get you back to him. Trust me, he's waiting for you."

Lisa melted. "You think so?"

"Yes, darling. Would you be able to help me? Just a couple of days so I can justify on the books that you've done some work? I'm sorry it has to be this way. And you can sleep here in my office. No more sleeping outside for you."

"But I didn't..."

"Yes you did dear. Have you looked at yourself? You'll sleep here. Come on, let me show you."

Lisa followed her down the hall and into her office.

"I'll bring you a mat and a... wait, no..." Mrs. Conner looked over at Lisa. "Actually, you know what?"

Lisa's eyes were heavy as she tried to listen.

"You'll sleep at my place. I rent an apartment just a few blocks away from here. Let's go there right now. You look like you could use a hot bath and a coffee. Or a nap."

Lisa was almost oblivious; she was so tired. Mrs. Conner took her hand and led her back through the hallway and towards the front door.

"Simon."

"Yes?"

"Can you handle things for a while? I'll be back in a bit."

"Sure."

Simon was in charge of the front desk and had gathered in everything that had just transpired over the last hour. His love and respect for Mrs. Conner had grown another measure deeper.

Simon had been there himself. When his family found his diary three years ago, they demanded that he leave the house, giving him only enough time to gather what was essential. "You say being gay is an abomination unto god, but he made this way!" he tearfully shouted back at them as he closed the door to the nest he'd been born into and, up until this day, had been nurtured and cared for.

Scared and tired, he stopped at the library to rest his feet and gather his thoughts. Sitting at the table, shaking in fear, he broke down and began sobbing when Mrs. Conner walked over to him and put her arms around him. After telling her what had happened, she led him out by the hand, asking Sarah at the front desk to watch things while she was gone. The next day, Simon had a new job at the library, and in a month, he had his own apartment. He stamped the back of the book and handed it to the man across the counter.

"That woman there..." pointing with his head towards Mrs. Conner, "remember her. She's a saint."

The man looked over at Mrs. Conner and then back to Simon.

"And she's not finished," Simon said.

The man drew his collar up around his neck as he prepared to walk back outside.

"Good to know," he said.

He turned, and then looked back at Simon.

Simon lifted his head and looked over at the door and, just for an instant, saw a beaked man with a tail smile back at him. He left the desk and ran to the front door, opened it, and looked outside. But he was gone. Simon slowly closed the door and returned to the front desk and did what he did best, suppress. This time, childhood visions.

Mrs. Conner opened the door and stepped aside to allow Lisa to enter first. The room was simple but warm.

"Come this way, dear," she said, as she led Lisa through the apartment and into the bathroom. "Lay your bag here for now. We'll wash your clothes tonight. I'm gonna run you a bath. Is that okay?"

"Yes, Mrs. Conner, thank you so much. I don't know what to say."

"Well, call me Gwendolyn. Or just Gwen. That's what my friends call me, and you're my friend, right?"

"Yes, but are you sure?"

"Yes, I'm sure. Now I'm gonna give you some privacy. Here's a towel, and if there's anything else you need just let me know."

"Who's that?" Lisa asked, looking up at a picture that hung in the hallway, just outside the bathroom door.

"That's Bobby. He was my husband."

Lisa waited.

"He died five years ago."

"His eyes remind me of Jaime's. Can I ask what happened?"

Gwen reached up into the cabinets, pretending to be looking for something while trying to chase away her tears. "He killed himself."

"Gwen, I told you about Jaime. Can I ask you to tell me about Bobby? You don't have to if you don't want to, but I can see you crying." Lisa turned the water off and sat on the edge of the tub. "Gwen?"

"He was so sweet, but he was troubled. There was a dark side to him that I never fully understood, but god knows I tried. He was real, and he made me feel so very safe, just like you were saying about Jaime. The last year of his life he started seeing people, visions. He would wake up in the middle of the night, or we would be out for a walk, or I would hear him arguing with someone in the other room, but when I walked in, he would look at me startled, and then try to pretend there was nothing going on."

"He saw people?" Lisa asked.

"Yes, that last year he did. He started drinking more and more. And then one weekend I left to go visit my parents. When I came home, I pulled into the parking garage. Occasionally some of the homeless folks would sleep there, and Bobby would wander downstairs and sit and drink with them."

Gwen walked over to the sink and splashed water on her face. "When I pulled in, he was sitting against the wall in our parking space in a pool of his blood. He'd cut his wrists. It had just happened. If I had come home an hour earlier, he might still be here." Gwen was sobbing.

Lisa stood up and walked over to Gwen and reached up to hug her. "I'm so sorry, Gwen."

Gwen buried her face in Lisa's neck.

Lisa hesitated to say anything but was too afraid not to. "Gwen."

"What dear?" she asked as they held each other

"Jaime sees people."

Gwen pushed away and looked sternly into Lisa's eyes. "What!"

"He sees people, Gwen. And then he tries to act like it's all okay, and that I have nothing to worry about. And he drinks a lot. And now I'm really scared. I'm scared, Gwen. I don't want to lose him." Lisa started crying. "Gwen, I have to get back to him. He's there all by himself and..."

Gwen pulled her back in. She was squeezing her so tight that Lisa struggled to breathe. "He's okay. He's okay. Do you hear me?"

"I don't know," Lisa said.

"He is." Gwen gently took Lisa by her shoulders, pushed her back, and looked into her eyes. "He's okay, dear. You take your bath and then sleep. I have a room just for you. Forget about working at the library. I'll get you on a bus tomorrow."

Gwen was balancing her dread and sense of urgency for Jaime with trying to keep Lisa calm. She took a hand towel and dried the tears from her face and backed herself out of the bathroom. "Take your bath, dear, and then you can snuggle up and sleep."

There was nothing she could do, so Lisa reluctantly pulled Jaime's shirt off and slid down into the water.

Jaime staggered half-asleep into his kitchen.

Lisa reached for the soap.

Jaime reached for a kitchen knife.

CHAPTER 15

My Name's Dito

Like the autumn leaves falling around her, Mary moved gracefully along the sidewalk, up the steps, and into the sanctuary. She quietly closed the swinging door behind her. It didn't matter though, the smell of campfire smoke that came in with her was just as distracting to those on the back pews as if she'd announced her entrance with trumpets and cymbals. It was something she was no longer mindful of. She was, however, mindful of being the only black person in attendance those mornings. She would come in shortly after the service had started and leave just before it ended, to spare the congregants from their awkward attempts at engaging with a homeless black woman.

She would immediately feel their eyes on her and hear the children whispering, but the hymns would soon soothe that all away. It was a middle-class white church, and the Appalachian music was far from what she had grown up with in the Delta, but when she closed her eyes, she could float right back to those familiar soulful sounds. That is, until the boy with that damn fiddle joined in.

To Jaime, Mary was the embodiment of the Christian narrative, the beautiful part of it, and it was genuine. Seemed to him, as though it could have been born of her, not the thing found in the churches that people were pretending at, but the ideal of it that they avoided. "It's like this," he had said to Jasmine one afternoon while Mary was in the shop. "If there is a heaven, and I'm sure there's not, but if there were, it would be filled with her." Jasmine followed Jaime's eyes as he watched Mary looking through the magazines.

Mary was trusting in the promise of something better. One day, she would inherit her heavenly mansion, but until then, she waited for her house under the shade of a magnolia tree, with flower gardens and bird feeders. Even though she was living in a tent, she somehow carried herself with such a graceful confidence, that one would've thought those promises had already come true.

Jaime knew what it meant to want and to thirst for something, but it wasn't the same. Mary's trust in something better brought her comfort now. Jaime would just stare at the ceiling and ache. "How do you reel in the future," he wondered as he ran his finger along the blade's edge. "How do you live like it's already here when it's not? And how can you be so sure that it's ever gonna be here anyway?" Jaime placed the knife just under his jawline and behind his ear, but then stopped and thought about one last cigarette, when he heard Ezra crawling out from the ceiling. He threw the knife across the kitchen in anger. "I'm not satisfying you now," he stuttered while taking a deep breath. "I'm not satisfying you!" he shouted towards the bedroom. He walked out the back door and slammed it behind him.

It was Sunday morning. He looked across the back lot at a family walking with bibles in hand, lit a cigarette to calm his nerves, and the thought of going to church crossed his mind. There were too many reasons not to, but dismissing his better judgment, he stepped back inside, grabbed his keys, and left.

He had to be at work by noon, so Jaime found a church near the shop. The service had already begun, and the parking lot was full, but there was room in an adjacent gravel lot, and from there he could slip in through the side door. All was calm in the surrounding neighborhood as he approached the red brick building. Through the stained-glass windows, he could hear the singing. He opened the door and slowly stuck his head inside. Stepping through, he was met with the repetitive refrain of "there's power in the blood," from within the sanctuary beyond the closed door to the right. Disturbing bloody images, like a fast-moving slideshow, flashed across his mind. He shook his head back into the moment and nearly walked out. But to his left was a narrow block-walled stairwell leading up to the second floor, and out of curiosity, he quietly closed the door behind him, climbed the dark stairway, and silently wandered down the hall to a small classroom at the end.

No one knew he was there, and he could hear everything. He looked around the room, sat down on a sofa, and closed his eyes. "This is different," he thought, remembering back to the days of being made to sit still on those hard-wooden pews. "Why don't they have sofas in church?" he asked the portrait of Jesus that hung on the opposite wall. The singing stopped, and the preacher was announced. Jaime put his legs up and turned over onto his side, just as he would back then. As soon as the preacher's opening prayer was over, his mother would pat her lap and he would lay his head where her soft cotton skirt stretched across her thighs. She would run her fingers through his hair until he fell asleep. Jaime laid on that short sofa, remembering his mother's hands, and waited for the prayer to end. It was long and verbose and was threatening to quench his Sunday morning curiosity.

Meanwhile, Mary played peekaboo with the small freckled-faced boy who was turned around in front of her. When the prayer mercifully ended, the boy's mother opened her eyes and pinched his leg, evoking a scream out of him that was loud enough to startle Jaime awake. He dug through his front pocket, pulled a cigarette out, and looked over at Jesus. "I guess this is why they don't have sofas in church." Remembering where he was, he put the cigarette back and reached for the bottle in his back pocket instead. Just as he was feeling the spirit rushing down this throat, the preacher cleared his throat and began, "As the spirit of the Lord is upon me, open your bibles to Jeremiah chapter twenty-nine and verse eleven." Jaime listened to the sound of hundreds of turning pages.

"For I know the plans I have for you," declares the Lord, "plans to prosper you and not to harm you, plans to give you hope and a future."

Jaime rolled over and violently coughed up the vodka that he'd inhaled while gasping at those words.

Mary closed her eyes and placed her hands over her melting heart.

Jaime listened as the preacher went on and on about these plans and all the good things god has in store for those who trust in him. He got up and began to pace the room. The preacher was getting worked up, and so was Jaime. "It's a curious thing though," Jaime stopped and said to the portrait of Jesus, "I mean, why should they be any more convinced that what he's saying is true, just because these guys shout spit at them with their hair flying all over the place?" He argued every point the preacher made, and finally shouted at the ceiling, "Wouldn't we be more convinced if your claims actually corresponded with reality?"

"No matter how bad you think you have it, god has a plan to prosper you!" the preacher said. "If you'll only trust in him!"

That was it. Jaime had heard enough. "She trusts in you godammit! Why are you letting her sleep in the woods?" He'd seen the make of cars in the parking lot, and as far as he could see, no one there needed any additional "prospering." Jaime grabbed the framed portrait from the wall, held it up to his face, and then threw it across the room. "Why am I even talking to you!" He stormed out and down the stairwell where he startled someone easing their way out the side door.

"Oh, sorry, I was just, uh…"

Jaime paused, sensing something and someone out of place. "I don't care."

She turned, her eyes drawing him in, and whispered, "Hey, you okay? You look upset."

"Not really."

"You wanna talk about it? My name's Dito. We should probably step outside, though, or they'll hear us."

"Sorry Dito, but right now I got something I need to take care of."

"Wait! That's the door to the..."

"I'm Jaime," he said, as he shoved open the door that led into the sanctuary and behind the pulpit. With eyes wide open, Dito dropped her bag and covered her gasp with both hands as she watched him storm the scene.

"Jaime!" she whispered loudly, "What are you... Oh my god, what the..." She laughed out loud and moved over to the other side of the doorway and out of view.

"What about my friend who sleeps in the woods every night!" Jaime shouted at the preacher, interrupting the sermon, and paralyzing the audience. "When do these plans come through for her? This makes no sense!" The sanctuary was in a state of shock. "Are you saying she has to endure this senseless suffering until she... what? Until what? Until when? What's gonna change? How's it gonna change, magic? She already trusts in this god you're talking about, but you'll all leave today and go home to your pretty houses while she walks back into those cold dark woods."

Jaime reached into his back pocket, pulled the bottle out, and took a drink, wiping his mouth with the sleeve of his white linen shirt. The congregation gasped. Dito was in disbelief, letting out short uncontrollable bursts of approving laughter from behind the half-opened door.

"This god you're singing about put her in that goddammed tent. So, when does this prospering deal come through for her?

Or does she have to die first? You're shouting about things you cannot defend. What about now! Why doesn't now matter!" He scanned the upper-middle-class white crowd and approached the pulpit when he heard her.

"Jaime!" Mary called out.

Jaime looked over towards the back of the sanctuary, and there she was, standing up in the corner.

"Mary?"

"Jaime! You get down from there right now!" Mary called out. "Get!"

Jaime stopped. He looked at the confused congregation, the stunned preacher, and then at Mary, "But..."

"No buts... You get down from there right now! You're not gonna do this in God's house!"

All heads were turning from back to front as they watched, some of them incensed, some of them feeling like they were hearing the gospel for the first time, and the rest just praying for Jesus to take the wheel.

Jaime hesitated. "But Mary..."

"I said get!"

Mary stepped out of the pew and started making her way down the aisle, and she sure as hell wasn't responding to an altar call. Jaime turned and walked back out the door he had burst in through.

"Jaime!" Dito said, grabbing him by his shirt until she tore the buttons. He was pulling away, trying to get out the door before Mary came after him.

"That was far out! But..."

"But what?"

"Wait, wait, wait," she said, holding him in place. "Alright, so here's the deal." She couldn't stop laughing. "If you're gonna advocate for someone, you should probably get their permission first."

Jaime turned his head away, fighting back tears over upsetting Mary.

"Hey, it's cool. You did a righteous thing, and I think you got a good heart. Anyway, come on, we gotta get out of here while they're still wondering what the hell just went down! Wait, you don't gotta coat?"

"No."

"But it's cold and wet out there!"

"I don't care."

"Jesus, Jaime," Dito rolled her eyes. "Come on. You gotta car?"

"Yeah."

"Does it have a heater?"

"Shut up, Dito."

Dito had organized and led protests against the Vietnam War a few years earlier. She'd helped smuggle draft dodgers across the Canadian border by arranging their bus tickets north. These tickets were unknowingly paid for in full by a church who, like the one she was currently pulling Jaime out of, left their tithes in the same unguarded place, at the same time, each Sunday. "Hey, they were doing the Lord's work, they just didn't know it," she would tell Jaime that evening at the campfire, pushing her shoulder against his to get a laugh out of him.

Dito wore a knit hat and a green army jacket with an upside-down American flag on the back, bell-bottom jeans, and boots. She had jumped a train heading south a couple of months ago rather than returning to school. She needed a break from the university scene. When the train stopped here, she got off to find food and rest. She had intended to go further the next day but met Bombay while looking for a discreet place to sleep for the night, and he invited her to come down to the campsite. A few days earlier, Misty had given in to her family's pleas to come home and had left her tent and blankets for whoever might need them next, and that was Dito. The following morning, while sitting around the fire over coffee and cigarettes, she got comfortable, made friends with those camping there, and gave up being in a hurry to move on.

"So how do you know Mary?" she asked, lifting his cigarettes out of his shirt pocket.

"I met her at the campsite where she stays, well, actually I first met her at the shop I'm working at."

"You've been to her campsite? That's where I stay too!"

"Wait, you stay there? I didn't see you, though."

"Yeah, every once in a while, I have the cash for a motel room. I don't mind the campsite, but it's nice to sleep in a bed sometimes. I'm going back tonight, though," she said, as she lit her cigarette. "Mary's cool, but I gotta feeling she's gonna let you have it next time you see her," she said laughing. "Where we goin' anyway?"

"To hell if we don't change our..."

Dito laughed and pushed his shoulder into the door, causing the car to swerve.

Jaime just managed to avoid the ditch, "Dito!"

"Sorry," she said, still laughing. "Yeah, we're probably going to hell in the end, but I didn't mean to almost send us there yet."

Jaime shook his head and laughed.

"So, about that scene though…"

"I didn't know she was gonna be there! I swear. I just decided to go this morning on impulse and, well, I mean, I didn't plan all that. It's just that, I don't know. It's not right. And yeah, she's not gonna be happy with me. Anyway, I gotta run by my place to get a jacket and then go to work."

"Yeah, you do. It's fuckin' freezing out here!"

Jaime had retreated into his head, consumed with the fear of seeing Mary.

"You're right, though," she said. "I'm traveling. I made this choice, but those folks are being bullied by a system that needs to come down." She slid her seat back and put her feet up on the dashboard. "We need a revolution," she said under her breath as she blew cigarette smoke out the window.

Jaime looked over at Dito and smiled.

"Hey, is there anywhere I can drop you?"

"Yeah, Havana," she said laughing. "Oh, I'll just go to the shop with you, if that's okay. I'm gonna pick up some supplies for the campsite. Wait, it's Cyril's shop, right?"

"Yeah, and that'd be alright. It won't take me long to grab a jacket."

Dito stared out the window. "Wait, I know who you are now. You're the guy Carol and Rookie were telling me about. Right? The guy who's gonna let us shop for free."

Jaime slightly shrugged his shoulders.

Dito leaned over and looked through the tapes on the floor. "Yeah, you're him."

Jaime tried to push the bottle of vodka back under his seat with the heel of his foot, but it was too late.

Dito looked up. "It's okay. I'm not gonna judge you, but those cops will."

Jaime's stare was broken by the sight. They were on his front porch. Again.

CHAPTER 16

It's All Random

With no window to the outside world, Lisa couldn't know how long she'd been in there, maybe days, maybe weeks. The sun and moon were hidden beyond the four block walls. There was no division of time, only the occasional moments of restless sleep. This cell, this thin lonely bed, this silence, felt like a tomb. Not since the night that Raymond first assaulted her had she considered killing herself. That night's thoughts were driven by anger, disgust, and shame. This was different. She'd lost all hope and faith in life itself. These were unfamiliar feelings. Was this it? Was she pulled from a web of fear and abuse into a moment of love and safety, only in the end to be crushed and discarded? She'd never see Jaime again; she'd never feel what it's like to be in love. And without hope, there is really no reason to go on.

The heavy lock to the cell door turned and Lisa awoke from a lethargic trance, "Why am I in here?" Lisa shouted. "I haven't done anything wrong!" The door opened and a guard came in holding the shirt, Jaime's shirt, that she was wearing when picked up by the police.

He held it up and pulled a lighter out of his pocket. "You see this?" he said, with a derisive laugh. Lisa leapt towards him to save it, but he shoved her back onto the bed, just like Raymond had done a hundred times before. He held the fire underneath the shirt until it went up in flames. "Get used to this place," he said, slinging it into the corner. "You're never getting out of here!" He walked out laughing and locked the door behind him. Lisa grabbed the bowl she'd been given in place of a toilet, ran over, and put the fire out. She held what was left of the shirt, sat in the corner, and cried.

"I haven't done anything wrong, why am I in here?"

She curled up into a fetal position and sobbed, "Why are you doing this to me?"

The overhead light was buzzing and flickering. Lisa looked over to her bed and saw a beaked man with a long tail sitting there. She sat up startled and held the shirt close to her heart. "Who are you! How'd you get in here?"

"Do it," he said, in a low and comforting voice.

"Do what?"

"You know."

Lisa drew her knees up to her chin. "You're the man who talks to Jaime, aren't you?"

"Do it."

"I'll do it if you promise to leave him alone."

"I won't say another word to him."

"What can I use though?"

He started twirling her sheet into a noose, when she heard a woman's voice outside the cell door. She turned and called out, "Nona?"

She looked back at the bed and he was gone.

"Lisa, it's Mrs. Conner, are you alright in there? I've come to check on you."

Jaime and Dito pulled into the small parking space behind the shop. "So, I don't gotta worry about you, right? I mean, your story about those cops on your front porch was a bit sketchy, and I'm not trying to get into your shit, but... yeah, I don't gotta worry about you, right?"

"I'm not a threat to you if that's what you're asking."

"Oh no, I'm not worried about that, I feel safe with you. I just don't wanna worry about you goin' away."

Jaime turned and looked at Dito. "I don't expect to be around much longer, but you don't gotta worry. It's not about those cops. Thanks, Dito, you're a good soul."

Dito looked down at the floor. "I don't know about that. I'm no saint, but..." looking up and out her window, "Hey," she tilted her head in the direction where Mary was staring at Jaime from around the corner of the building. He leaned forward and saw her, they made eye contact, and Jaime collapsed back into his seat with a sigh, "I'm so fucked."

"It'll be okay. Mary's cool. Go talk to her."

"Yeah, I will. I guess I deserve whatever I'm gonna get, though."

Dito pushed his shoulder into the door. "Just go. I'm gonna grab some things from the shop," she stuck her head back inside before walking off, "Git!"

"Shut up Dito!"

Dito laughed. "You shut up! And we're not finished."

Jaime looked over at Mary, and then back up at Dito. "What?"

"Don't go anywhere until we have the chance to talk some more. Okay?"

Jaime got out and looked over the top of the car at Dito. "Okay."

"Go talk to her Jaime, it'll be alright." Dito paused and looked down the tracks.

Jaime's eyes followed. "They're calling you, aren't they?"

Dito walked over to Jaime and wrapped her arms around his neck from behind. "We're all being called by something, Jaime. The trick, I think, is to be honest with yourself. Who's calling you, why, and where to. Where to, Jaime? That one place you can't come back from?" She raised up on her toes and spoke into his ear, "Don't go there yet, I don't care who's calling you."

Jaime took a deep breath and was ready to tell her everything.

"Hey! Guess who's calling you now," Dito said before he could get a word out.

"Who?"

"Mary."

Jaime sighed, "Jesus, I don't wanna do this."

Dito laughed hard, hugged him tight, and then let him go.

Jaime looked across the parking lot.

"Git!" Dito laughed.

Jaime side-eyed her. "That's getting old, Dito."

She gave him a gentle push in the back. "You're gettin' old."

Jaime shook his head and laughed.

"I'm going into the shop. I'll catch up with you after."

Jaime lit a cigarette and walked over to Mary. Without a word spoken, she took his arm and led him around to the other side of the building and to the buckets.

Mary pulled hers up to face Jaime. She reached over and took his hands. "It doesn't have to make sense to you, Jaime. I can't explain it, this hope I have. I didn't put it there. I didn't dream it up. It's just there. Underneath all of your anger and sadness, you have a sweet heart, and I want you to be happy. Why can't you be happy, love?"

"I don't know. I didn't put these feelings here, either Mary. I didn't ask for this. I don't wanna be this way." Jaime looked away with tears welling up. "It's him."

"It's who?"

"He used to come into my room at night when I was a child, and..."

"Did your father..."

"No, no, no! It was this... never mind, Mary. I don't wanna talk about it."

Mary slid her bucket over next to his and put her arm around him. Jaime turned and buried his face into her neck. Before he could come undone, Mary pulled away and grabbed him by his shoulders. She followed his eyes with hers until he surrendered contact. "Hey, you know what?"

"What?"

"When I get my house, it's gonna have flower gardens everywhere. I'm gonna have a big ol' welcome mat out front, and I'm gonna have all my friends over on Sunday afternoons for dinner. You know, I'm a pretty good cook. Oh! And I make a really good pot roast! I think I'll have it painted blue, whatdya think? You like blue?"

"What? The pot roast?"

Mary grabbed his face and laughed out loud. "No, the house, silly."

Jaime shrugged his shoulders.

Mary pulled a tissue from her coat pocket. "Where'd you get those green eyes?" she asked. "They're so pretty. Don't cover them up with tears."

Mary gently pulled his glasses off and pressed the tissue into his eyes, blotted them dry, and then put the tissue away. "I think there's more to all this. I know you have a troubled soul darling, but I think maybe your heart's breaking?"

Jaime hung his head and nodded. "I messed up, Mary. I let her go."

"When Bombay asked you the other night about your friend, I noticed that everything changed for you. Is it her?"

He nodded.

"You love her, don't you."

He nodded again. "But I don't know if she loves me like I love her."

"Who were you talking to that night?"

"Nobody."

Mary half-smiled. "Jaime." She looked down and shuffled her feet across the gravel. "It's okay, sometimes we need to hold things in. But when the time's right, you gotta let it out, darlin'. It'll just eachyou up inside."

Jaime stood up and began to pace. "She said she was gonna write me."

"How long has it been?"

"She left on Thursday."

"Well then, you should be getting that letter any day now."

"When I do, I'm gonna go find her. It should have her sister's return address on it."

"There you go, you're gonna get your friend back, and I'm gonna get my pretty blue house."

Jaime walked back towards Mary, but then turned and noticed a moth desperately fighting for its life in the spider web spun across the shop's drainage pipes. He stopped, wrapped his arms around the support pillar, and wondered.

"Hope," he thought. "Does that moth hope? Is there someone watching us, like I'm watching her? Does she hope in something or someone rescuing her from the despair? Is someone or something gonna reach out and rescue us from ours?"

He pressed his forehead against the pillar. "I doubt it."

Jaime let go, walked over, and gently pulled the moth from the web, and set her free. She fluttered past his face and landed on the handrail of the small steps at the back door.

"It's random," he thought, looking down at the moth. "I just happened to reach you before the spider did. It's all random. We're moving our pieces around the board to a roll of the dice." The back door opened, interrupting his thoughts, and breaking his stare. It was Cyril. Mary looked away.

"There you are! You're supposed to be working. It's past twelve. Get inside or you can find yourself another job."

Cyril rolled his newspaper. It was the moth's turn at the dice. Bad roll. Cyril stuck his head back inside after scraping his paper down the edge of the handrail. "Jasmine! You're forgetting to turn this back light out in the mornings. It's attracting moths." Jaime looked down and watched her struggle through one last attempt to move her broken wings, and then up at Cyril. He wanted to take him to the river, but walked past him in disgust, and on through the back door.

Jasmine turned. "Jaime! You're here. I was starting to get worried about you."

"And you stay out of my shop!" Cyril barked at Mary as he opened his car door.

"Yes sir," Mary replied.

"Yeah, I'm here," Jaime said, as he gave Jasmine a hug and looked to see what was left in the coffee pot.

"He's gone," Jasmine said, as she slightly opened the back door to be sure. "Let's get these guys in here. I'll make another pot of coffee. It looks like you could do with some, too."

She opened wide the back door and motioned for Mary and Dito to come in. Bombay, Carol, and Rookie had all arrived too. They shuffled in like moths with broken wings and waited for Jasmine to make the coffee. Jaime closed the door behind them.

Mrs. Conner opened the bathroom door. "Lisa!" She grabbed a towel and shook her by the arm. "Lisa! Wake up, sweetie. I'm glad I came home for lunch. You can't be falling asleep in the bathtub!"

Lisa slowly opened her eyes, sat up, and wrapped the towel around her shoulders. "My shirt! Where's my shirt!"

"It's right here, sweetie." Gwen picked it up from the floor beside her. "See, it's right here. You want me to wash it for you? I was gonna do some laundry."

"No! Don't wash it! Never wash it!" she said. "Give me it. I need it. I need to hold it."

"But you'll get it..."

"Just give it to me, Gwen. It's Jaime's. Please, I just need to hold it. I had a really bad dream and I need to know he's near. I need to feel and smell him."

Gwen handed the shirt to Lisa. "When can I go Gwen? Can I go tomorrow?" Lisa asked.

"Yes, I'll get you on a bus tomorrow, dear. It's gonna be okay. Now dry yourself off, and put your shirt on, and I'll make you some lunch."

"How much are these food containers?" Dito called out to Jasmine from the far side of the shop.

"Everything's free when Jaime's here," Rookie called back.

Jasmine shook her head and laughed.

"Rookie, goddammit!" Carol grabbed him by the arm and started to drag him out the back door, just as two police officers were coming through the front.

"Mr. Felts, we need to speak with you for a moment," one of the officers said.

Dito stepped aside. All eyes, including Carol and Rookie's, whose exit was interrupted, were exchanging looks of contempt with the police officers. They were all too familiar with each other.

"What do you want?" Jaime asked.

"We're still looking for Miss Harris. We entered her place with a search warrant this morning, and her closet and dresser drawers were full of clothes, there were personal items scattered around like jewelry, toiletries, and a diary."

Jaime froze at the thought of there being a diary, and that they had it.

"There is other evidence that seems to indicate one of two things, either you're telling us the truth, that you put her on a bus to Oklahoma City, and by the way, the police are looking for her there, or she's still around. If you put her on a bus, why did she leave all these things behind? Was she in a hurry to get out of town? And if the other is true, and you're hiding her, we'll find out, and you'll be charged as an accomplice to this murder."

Bombay looked over at Jaime and then at the officer. "Please, most honored constable, my friend here..."

"Be quiet you drunk!" the officer said, looking sternly into Bombay's eyes.

Jaime was incensed. Jasmine and Dito cut their eyes with looks that could kill. The others had grown accustomed to these slurs.

"So, is there anything else you may have forgotten to tell us Mr. Felts?" the other officer asked.

Jaime took his cigarettes out of his shirt pocket and pulled one out. "Yeah, there is one thing that I neglected to tell you, but it just slipped my mind."

"What's that?" the officer asked.

Jaime curled his hand around his lighter, furrowed his eyebrows to focus, and without looking up from the tip of his cigarette he said, "Go fuck yourselves."

Carol, Bombay, Mary, and Rookie all looked down into their cups, trying to suppress their collective laughter. Not Dito. She collapsed onto the magazine rack, with her forehead shaking back and forth on her arm, while Jasmine crossed hers, tilted her head, and raised her eyebrows at the officers with a, "Well?"

They looked at Jasmine, and then back over at Jaime. "You're still a suspect, Mr. Felts," the officer replied. "Don't be too sure of yourself. We're not convinced that Miss Harris could've gotten Mr. Gillis into that river without some help. Let's see what this diary tells us, maybe it'll change your attitude," he said, slapping it in the palm of his hand. They scanned the familiar faces of those they'd spun around and handcuffed over and over again. "I'm sure we'll be seeing all of you soon," one of them said as they walked out.

"So it's true?" Mary asked, "Raymond Gillis was killed?"

"We heard that too!" Carol said, with Rookie nodding in agreement. "I mean, I don't blame her though. I remember when I stayed at the mission, how Raymond would beat her up all the time. I remember one time in the courtyard he had her by the neck, and I thought he was gonna strangle her to death right there!"

"Yeah, that one staff guy stopped him, or I think he would've," Rookie said.

"Wait, they were living in the other side of your duplex, Jaime? Next door to you?" Dito asked.

Jaime nodded his head.

"How did they end up there?"

"Raymond got a job as a plumber or something," Carol said, "and got out of the mission. I didn't know he was living next door to you, though, Jaime. Anyway, Lisa went with him. We all tried to talk her out of it, but she went anyway."

Dito straightened the magazines. "So, I guess you would've known," she said, without looking back.

"Known what?" Jaime asked.

"Known that he was abusing her."

Jaime quenched his cigarette in his coffee cup. "She didn't do it."

He walked over to the counter. "I gotta do some inventory guys. Y'all stay as long as you want, but I gotta get to work. Jasmine, can you hand me the clipboard?"

Jasmine looked at him like he had just asked for a moon rock.

Jaime reached past her, grabbed a clipboard that probably hadn't been touched in years, and placed his pencil in position to write, but had no idea what to do next. He just needed all eyes off of him. And it worked. For all but two.

He could see Dito looking at him out of the corner of her eyes. He turned, and Jasmine was looking up at him while taking a drink from her coffee.

He knew they knew, but the show had to go on.

CHAPTER 17

How Do You Know He's a Dishwasher

"Hey, I thought about doing some eggs and bacon for lunch. I was running late for work this morning and didn't eat breakfast. What do you think?"

"That sounds good to me, Gwen. Actually, anything sounds good to me. I'm starving."

"Okay! I think I've got everything we need. I'll do some toast and potatoes, too. You like ketchup with your eggs?"

Lisa stopped drying her hair and looked out from underneath the towel. "Ketchup?" she asked.

"Yeah, it's a thing."

Lisa laughed, "Uh, no it's not, Gwen. Jaime's the only person I've ever known to pour ketchup over eggs, and it actually hurts to watch."

"Well, you'd better get used to it, dear. You're going back to him tomorrow, and you two are gonna be eating a lot of breakfasts together."

Lisa blushed, "Oh Gwen, I can't wait," she turned and studied herself in the mirror, "I hope he loves me like I love him."

"Get out of that mirror! You're beautiful, Lisa. Now let's go have some eggs and ketchup."

Lisa wrapped herself in her towel and followed Gwen towards the kitchen, rolling her eyes and making a gagging gesture. Gwen turned around and they filled the hallway with laughter.

"Hey Gwen, what time do you get off tonight?" Lisa asked, standing at the door to the kitchen while still drying her hair.

"Normally six, but I'm gonna take off early today. I should be home around five. Wanna curl up on the sofa and find a movie to watch?"

"I'd love that! I noticed there's a shop around the corner. I have a few dollars left. I could pick up some vegetables and rice if you want. I know how to make a really good vegetable soup. If that sounds good to you."

"You don't have to do that. You're my guest."

"I want to! Besides, it'll take my mind off things today. Do you mind me making myself at home in your kitchen?"

"Not at all, but just charge the groceries to my account. Oh! And how about some popcorn for the movie?"

"Sure! Sounds like we're having a girl's night," she said pulling her hair back. "I've never had a girl's night."

"Oh, it's a girl's night alright. Do you like red or white wine?"

"Um, I'm okay."

"I'm sorry Lisa, I shouldn't have…"

"It's okay, Gwen. It's just that alcohol can trigger bad feelings for me. My father hit me when he was drunk. Raymond all but killed me when he was drunk. I think the only reason he didn't was so he'd have someone to beat up on the next day. There were times..." Lisa stared into her cup.

"There were times, what?" Gwen asked.

Lisa looked at Gwen. "There were times when I actually thought about killing him for the things he did to me." Lisa set her coffee down, flipped her hair over, and began running her fingers through the tangles. "He hurt me, but the humiliation was almost more than I could stand. I knew Jaime heard me screaming and crying from next door, and he tried to help me, but I was too scared to let him. I was afraid of putting him in Raymond's path. He didn't deserve to be hurt too."

The kitchen went quiet.

Lisa was reliving those images while Gwen was trying to chase them away.

"Anyway, those days are gone forever. I'm safe with Jaime, even when he's drinking. I just don't like that he needs it. I don't understand that, Gwen. I know there are so many things I don't know about him, but he's not a drunk, and he's not mean when he's been drinking. Actually, he relaxes and talks, and it's really nice to hear him talk, but when he's had too much, he starts to fade and seems kinda confused about things. But he's still really sweet and gentle. I don't know. I guess I just worry about him."

"I understand," Gwen said. "I remember those days with my Bobby. But it's not good for those that struggle like he did, and your Jaime does. Drinking can embolden them. It can give them the courage to do things that those of us who love them don't want them to do."

"What do you mean?"

"I think drinking releases one's inhibitions. In other words, it brings out who a person really is. I'm no expert, but it seems to me to be true. And that's why I think my Bobby did what he did. He may have struggled with life, but I don't think he would've ever used that razor on himself if he hadn't been drinking."

Lisa pressed the towel into her face and then threw it back over her hair with a deep breath. "Let's talk about something else, Gwen. Hey! Get those eggs cookin' and I'll get the ketchup out," she said, nervously forcing a laugh.

Gwen walked over and wrapped her arms around her. "I'm scared Gwen," she whispered. "Am I gonna get there in time?" Both were reluctant to let go, but Gwen pulled away enough to look Lisa in her eyes. "I don't know dear, but I think he loves you, and I think he's waiting to hear from you. I know it's hard, but try not to worry. I have a good feeling about you two."

Lisa hugged Gwen's neck tight. "Why are you so nice to me?"

"I honestly don't know that either," Gwen said with a laugh. "You're just so adorable. I like seeing you smile, it lights up the room, and I want you to see your dreams come true. I really think it'll be okay. Let's trust Nona." Gwen grabbed Lisa by her shoulders. "Okay, so, scrambled or fried?"

"What?" Lisa asked, as she pulled away.

"Your eggs. Do you like them scrambled or fried?"

"Did you say 'Nona'?"

"No dear, I asked if you'd like your eggs scrambled or fried. Who's Nona?"

Lisa looked away, smiled, and gathered herself back into the moment. "Jaime likes his scrambled, so I'd better get used to that," Lisa answered with a laugh.

Gwen looked over her glasses from the stovetop, and before she could get the words out of her mouth, Lisa assured her, "I know, I know, I don't have to do and like everything that Jaime does. I've just never been in love before. And besides smarty pants, it's easier to just make one kind or the other!" she said, crossing her arms and tilting her head.

Gwen remembered those days. She smiled and began breaking the eggs over the edge of the skillet. Lisa flipped her hair over in the towel and began humming her favorite song from Jaime's records. Gwen seasoned the eggs with the salt from a tear.

"Why can't you just leave it here and we'll walk? It's just down there, under that bridge."

"I know where it is, Carol, but what if somebody steals it?"

"I don't think anybody's gonna steal that car, Jaime."

"What are you trying to say? What's wrong with my car!"

"And besides, you told us you park it on a hill most of the time in case you have to roll it off and jump-start it."

"But they're not gonna know that!"

"If they steal it, they're gonna have to..."

Jasmine cut in, "Hey you two, this is a fascinating conversation, but can we go? Jaime, I really think it'll be fine. I've left mine here a hundred times before, and..."

"Yeah and look at her car."

Jaime closed his eyes. "Carol."

"Yeah?"

"So help me, sweet Jesus, if my car's gone when we get back..." Jasmine covered his mouth and spun him around towards the bridge.

"Uh, Jaime..."

"What now, Carol?"

"You need to take that bottle out of your back pocket."

"Why?"

"Cause, you're not allowed to have alcohol at the service."

"What? Jesus turned water into..."

"They have cops there and if they catch you, they'll arrest you," Rookie said.

Jaime dropped his shoulders, leaned his head back, and sighed. "How long must I ..."

Mary lifted the branches of a bush next to the sidewalk. "Jaime! It's okay! You're not Jesus. Just hide it under here and you can get it on our way out."

Jaime stopped, twisted the cap off, and flushed it down his throat. He wiped his mouth with his sleeve and threw the empty bottle as far as he could.

Carol looked at the others and then back at Jaime. "Or you could do that."

Mary closed her eyes with a sigh and then grabbed Jaime by the arm. "Come on. Something tells me we're gonna be carrying you before this night's over."

As they approached the bridge the music started, and a woman with a mic launched into a far too enthusiastic version of, *I'll Fly Away*, prompting Jaime to reply under his breath, "Please do."

"What?" Mary asked.

"Nothing," Jaime said.

"You gonna be okay, boy? Look here, I love you, but I don't have to worry about you giving us another performance, do I? Some of these folks are gonna recognize you from this morning."

Dito let out a laugh from behind. "Oh my god! I would pay to see…"

Mary turned around. "Dito!"

"Sorry, Mary."

"Lord, you two are thick as thieves."

Dito shrugged her shoulders.

"So tell me the truth, Jaime. You've already had too much to drink, and I'm not stepping into this service until you promise me that you're not gonna cause another scene."

"But what if they make me mad again?"

"Jaime."

"Okay, I won't make a scene."

Dito took Jaime's hand and held him back as Mary and the others crossed the railroad tracks and into the fenced event. "I got this Mary," she said.

The opening prayer was over, and the woman with the mic launched into an absurdly loud rendition of *When the Roll Is Called Up Yonder*, so Dito had to raise her voice and speak directly into Jaime's ear. "Are you okay?"

Jaime scanned the scenes around him in reverse order, and back into Dito's eyes. "No Dito, I'm never okay, but I won't repeat this morning. You don't gotta worry about that."

"I'm not worried about that, trust me, I'm worried about you. You see things, don't you?"

"I'm okay."

"Jesus, Jaime! You just said you're never... never mind." Dito opened her arms, lifted herself on her toes, and pulled him in. "You don't gotta talk about it, but if you ever wanna."

"Why are you shouting?" Jaime asked.

Dito buried her face into his neck, shook her head, laughed, and hugged him tighter. He was impossible. "Let's go get in line, Jaimz. Just stay with me. I'll keep you outta trouble tonight."

Jaime looked at her.

"Nah, we'll still probably end up in trouble," She said with a laugh. "But stay with me anyway. Trouble's always better when spread around. Right?"

"I guess."

The atmosphere was heavy with sinners and saviors, but not a saint to be found, until Jaime looked over at Mary. It was as though the universe rose and bowed in reverence to her entrance, like to a queen. No one did, of course, she was homeless. But Jaime could sense the sun, the moon and stars, the wind, trees, and the oceans giving way to her presence. And yet there she was, under a filthy bridge, sitting in a metal chair at a folding table, eating from a tray. The image hypnotized him.

"Sorry, I'm getting a tray for both me and my friend, he's deaf and mute," Dito said, pushing her elbow into Jaime's side, and cutting her eyes at him. "Do. You. Want. Gravy. On. Your. Mashed. Potatoes?" she asked him, as though he needed to read her lips.

Jaime looked away from Mary, and stared a hole through Dito, fighting back a grin. "Okay, I was distracted for a few minutes," he thought to himself, "but we can do this." He then made some nonsensical gestures with his hands.

Dito turned her head, but it was too late, she was done. Jaime rescued the tray while Dito stumbled away from the table laughing uncontrollably.

Jaime looked at the food servers, shrugged his shoulders, and made his way over to Mary's table, with Dito staggering in laughter behind him. When one of the volunteers came over to the table and asked Jaime in sign language, something that no one understood, Dito spewed her tea into Jaime's face, and nearly fell backwards in her chair, while the others sat confused.

Jaime dried himself and was starting to settle in to finding a rare appetite when Ezra sat down beside him.

"What are you doing here!"

All eyes were on Jaime.

"No you don't! Shut up! You don't know what's in her diary. I fuckin' hate you! I'm glad you stepped out in front of that train! Leave me alone! I'll do it when I'm ready."

Jaime raked his tray onto the ground and stormed away from the table.

They all looked at one another, wondering what to do, as Jaime walked out of the light and down the railroad tracks that led into the dark woods. Bombay stood up. "He's being disturbed. I'll go care for him."

Bombay kindly and respectfully approached Jaime who was sitting on a rail in the dark, with his head in his hands. "My friend, can I sit alongside you?"

Jaime looked up. "Yeah, you can sit with me, Bombay."

"I'll be right back." Bombay walked further down the tracks. Jaime watched him in the black night go down to his knees. He continued watching until Bombay finally stood up, and followed the rail back to Jaime, and sat down beside him. He took the cap off of the bottle of mouthwash and offered Jaime the first drink.

"You go ahead," Jaime said, gently pushing Bombay's hand away.

"I understand. The first time is not easy, my friend, but I've found it much cheaper than vodka."

He looked over at Jaime. "It also makes my breath sparkle."

Bombay smiled as Jaime couldn't help but chuckle.

He took a few drinks while they sat in silence, and then asked, "What is a diary?"

Jaime pulled his cigarettes out of his shirt pocket and offered Bombay one.

"I'd rather not, but please, you enjoy."

"It's a book Bombay," he said, as he paused to light his cigarette. "It's a book where you write down your secret thoughts."

Bombay took another drink and looked up for the stars. "So, it's the book where your friend would chronicle her love for you?"

"Why do you say that?" Jaime asked.

"Jaime," this was the first time Bombay had called Jaime by his name. "Sometimes I feel as though I'm sitting on a high mountain top, and I know nothing at all about this mountain, but I see all that is going on in the valley below. Sometimes I wish I didn't. Sometimes I wish I could close my eyes, but I can't. I was put on this mountain against my will…"

Jaime could see Bombay's bloodshot eyes welling with tears. "Does the mouthwash help?" he asked tenderly.

Bombay clenched his jaws and tried his best to stop the tears. "No, Jaime, it only shines bright lights onto the valley. But, please, listen to me. I know your friend loves you desperately. I've seen it from this high place. You must believe me."

Jaime shuffled his feet in the gravel. "I love her so much, Bombay, and I wanna believe she loves me the same, but then, what does it all matter anyway?"

Bombay took Jaime's hand in one and calmed it with his trembling other. "I've seen two small, lonely mountain streams converge into one, and it's fullness springs life. The waters from each swell and offer a place for happy fish to flourish."

It was Jaime's turn to cry.

"This stream, this joining of waters, it doesn't have to go anywhere, it can rest and become a deep pool that hides the evils of this world. Can you imagine that my friend?"

Jaime pictured Raymond sinking and nodded his head.

Bombay slid down onto his back, using the rail as a pillow. He lifted his knees, clasped his hands across his chest, and looked up at the night sky. "Who is this man, this one who washes dishes and taunts you?"

Jaime put his cigarette out and stood up. "How do you know he's a dishwasher?"

Bombay looked over at him. "I've seen him from the high mountain, and I don't like him."

"Another time Bombay. I'm going back to join the others. What will you do?"

"I'll lie here for a time, and then make my way to our encampment. I don't require forgiveness."

"What do you mean?"

"At the end of our banquet, those wearing tuxedos ask us to come to the front for prayers to Jesus. They say he can stop us from drinking, or possibly, offer forgiveness to those of us who can't. I see my friends cry and promise him they'll change their ways, only to return to their home in the woods and drink, while the fancy ladies and gentlemen drive away until the next banquet."

Jaime cast his eyes down the tracks and back. "Yeah, you certainly don't require forgiveness, Bombay. Listen, I'm gonna join the others, you sure you won't come with me?"

"Not now. You go."

Jaime started back down the tracks towards the service when Bombay called out.

"Don't let him deceive you tonight my friend!"

CHAPTER 18

It's Dark and Intense

"Wanna stay with us tonight, Jaime?" Carol asked. Jaime's car hadn't been stolen, and she made sure that he knew it, as they approached the shop. "I guess they couldn't roll it off."

Jaime cut his eyes at her.

Rookie grinned and looked over at him, but before Jaime could respond, Dito grabbed him by his shoulders from behind.

"Yeah, you probably don't need to be driving," she said, while sliding her hand down into his front pocket and taking his cigarettes out.

"Does anyone around here buy cigarettes?" he asked, "I mean..."

"Oh, shut up Jaime, I'm pretty sure you don't actually *buy* these," Dito said laughing.

Jaime turned around and tried snatching them from Dito's hand, but she was faster. "Hey, anyone else want one?" she asked, holding Jaime back at arm's length.

"Yeah!" everyone said. They passed the pack around and back to Dito who returned it to Jaime empty.

"Jasmine, can you let me in the shop for a minute? I think I left something in there."

Jasmine rolled her eyes. "Really? You forgot something Jaime? Just wait here, I'll go in and get your cigarettes."

"We can't buy cigarettes, Jaime," Rookie put the word 'buy' in quotation marks with his fingers, "because you keep them behind the counter."

"I'll fix that," he said, as he sat down on the curb.

Dito sat down beside him.

"I like it when you laugh."

Jaime crossed his arms and held his opposite shoulders as though he were in a straitjacket. While leaning forward, he found his eyes reflected back in a puddle of water between his feet.

"I don't really laugh much."

"Yeah, I've kind of picked up on that. But I know when you find things funny. I can see it in your eyes."

Everyone was waiting for Jasmine to come out from the shop with cigarettes, and for Bombay to join up.

Dito reached over and gently pulled Jaime's arms off of his shoulders and put her arm around him. "You don't gotta hold yourself. There's plenty of folks around here who'll hold you."

Jaime turned and wrapped his arms around Dito.

"So yeah," she said, "you don't laugh much, but I think you really like to make others laugh, don't you."

"When I see people laugh, they look like they're in heaven, and I love that for them."

"Jaimz."

He pulled out of her embrace.

"Where are you?"

Jaime cut his eyes away.

"Are you already in hell?"

Jaime watched as the plastic lid to a paper cup blew passed them and unicycled down the road.

"Dito, someone once told me that hell was nothing more than Jesus describing the trash that continuously burned outside the city. So yeah, I'm trash, and I'm continuously burning."

They both sat in silence.

"You wear a cross."

"Yeah, it was my mother's. She believed it would protect me."

"From?"

"Demons."

"Does it?"

"They haven't gotten me yet."

Dito reached over and lifted it from his chest. "I like it."

She leaned over and whispered into his ear, "Stay with Bombay tonight, Jaimz. I think it'll be good for you."

He looked over at her, took the cross off from around his neck and began to place it around hers.

She pushed it back.

"Not yet. You never know. And you don't need to be alone tonight. And please, don't drive."

"Okay, but what do I do with my car? What if somebody…"

"Jaime! I swear to god if you…"

"You shouldn't swear to god, Dito. If it doesn't come true, you'll never go to heaven."

Dito chuckled and shook her head.

"What the hell's wrong with you Jaimz? What rocket ship did you come in on?"

She took his hand and quoted Smokey Robinson. "*Now they're some sad things known to man; But ain't too much sadder than the tears of a...*"

Jaime stared into the puddle.

"Hey," she said nudging his shoulder with hers. "I'm sorry. I don't think you're a clown."

Jaime turned his head away.

"A little grease paint looks good on you though," Dito said, with an empathetic smile. "It hides your sadness."

Jaime nodded his head.

"We all wear it at times, Jaime. It's just that most of us don't wanna admit to it."

"Dito."

"What is it, Jaimz?"

"I know I'm still young, but why do I feel like, it just feels like... why have I been alone for so long?"

"I don't know, Lisa. You're still so young though."

"It feels long, Gwen."

"It does, doesn't it? Loneliness feels so long, and happiness never feels long enough. Come over and sit on the sofa, dear. I truly don't know why you've been alone for so long. Come over here."

Lisa put her soup bowl on the counter and walked over to the sofa. Gwen patted her lap and Lisa curled up and laid her head on it.

"I'm sorry. I feel like I'm hard work for you. Let's watch this movie."

"It's okay. You're not hard work. What's got you thinking about this?"

"I don't know. I guess I'm just getting more and more nervous as tomorrow gets closer, and I think it's 'cause tomorrow means that the loneliness either ends forever or goes on forever."

"That's understandable."

Gwen set her elbow on the arm of the sofa and rested her cheek on her closed hand.

"As much as I'd like to, I can't ease your fears about it, dear heart. But when I have moments like this, I like to go to the worst case and sit there for a minute. It's like, okay, this is the worst it can get."

Lisa nodded.

"So, worst case, Jaime doesn't love you like you love him..."

Lisa turned, buried her face, and shook her head.

"But you live next door to him, and he holds you every night, and makes you breakfast every morning."

She looked up from Gwen's lap.

"He could grow to love me."

"Of course he could, sweetie. Remember, this is the worst."

Lisa nodded again.

"What's the best?"

"He runs to meet me at the bus station, and grabs me up and kisses me, and tells me he wants to spend the rest of his life with me."

Gwen laughed.

"Well, he's not expecting you, so the running through the bus station isn't likely, but I think you got the rest of it about right."

Lisa smiled and curled up tighter. Gwen pulled the shawl off from the back of the sofa and covered her with it.

"Gwen?"

"What dear?"

"How did you become a librarian?"

"Oh, Lisa. It was years and years ago. I was in San Francisco and was hired on, just like Simon, to work the front desk. The head librarian was a good man. He was retiring in a couple of years, and he took the time to teach me and train me, so I could take his place. I didn't know anything about running a library!" she said with a laugh.

Lisa pulled the shawl from her face. "Do you think I could be a librarian?"

"Yeah, Lisa. I do. It just takes time though."

"I got time."

"I know you do."

"I wanna do something with my life. I don't wanna get back to Tennessee and just sit around in the house all day. You know what I mean?"

"I know exactly what you mean."

"I watch you in the library, and I think I'd like to do that too. I know it's a lot of work, but it's important what you do. And you get to help people too, and I'd like to do that. Do you really think I could do it?

"I really do, Lisa. The first step is to get your foot in the door. I'll give you a letter of recommendation that you can take back with you.

"But I haven't done any work, Gwen."

"It'll be a letter of personal recommendation. Trust me, it'll make a difference."

Lisa closed her eyes and smiled, but then raised up. "So, what's this movie about?"

"You've never seen *Roman Holiday*?"

"No, what's it about?"

"It's a love story. It's cute."

"Oh. Well, I've not really seen a lot of movies before."

Gwen stood up and walked over to the TV set and started turning the channels. "Oh! Here we go, *The Sound of Music* is on, much better! Have you seen it?"

"No."

"Well, you have to see this movie, Lisa. It's wonderful."

She turned the lights off, curled up into the corner of the sofa, and Lisa laid her head in Gwen's lap before jumping back up. "Wait! The popcorn!"

Jasmine came out and handed Jaime his cigarettes.

"Here, now I'm going home to get some sleep. You should really do the same."

"He's coming with us tonight," Carol said.

"An even better idea."

"Mary, you're glowing. What's goin' on? Who was that woman with the notebook you were sitting with tonight?" Imani asked.

Dito and Jaime stood up. Dito grabbed him by his shirt and pulled him close.

"You're not alone, Jaime."

"Dito…"

"What is it Jaimz?"

"Here comes Bombay," Rookie said.

"Later."

Dito let go and straightened his shirt. "We're not finished, okay?"

"Okay."

Jaime turned and then looked into Mary's eyes. Imani was right-she was glowing.

"Let's go on down the hill and get the fire going. I'll tell you all about it," Mary said.

Jaime took a few bags from Dito's hands. "I can carry some of these. Did you get everything you needed?"

"I did. Thanks, Jaime. How do y'all get away with this? I mean, doesn't that creep notice?"

"Jasmine takes care of it. She just tells him that the shop was shorted when the deliveries come in, and then she adjusts the books to show it."

"Cool. But he'll catch on to y'all one day, dontcha think?"

"I doubt me and Jasmine will still be here by the time he does. She'll be going back to Memphis sometime soon."

"And you?"

"I'll be going back to Pluto."

Dito wilted with laughter. "I'm sure they miss you there, Jaimz." She punched him on the shoulder. "You're a Scorpio, aren't you?"

"Yeah, how'd you know?"

"Thought so, I'm feelin' it. I mean, it's pretty obvious, Jaime. And this is your season."

"I don't know what that means."

"It's dark and intense, Jaime. Especially for all you guys from Pluto," she said laughing.

Jaime shook his head and turned away. Dito reached for his belt loop and pulled him along the sidewalk towards the church on the hill. Mary caught up from behind and whispered between them, "I'm getting my house."

They both stopped and turned.

"Shhhhh, don't say anything yet. I wanna tell everyone together."

Mary walked on ahead and caught up with Imani, while Jaime and Dito slowed, looking at one another, but not knowing what to say.

"Maybe it's true," Jaime said.

"Maybe what's true?" Dito asked.

"God. Maybe there's really somebody, somewhere, looking out for her."

"I don't know."

"Yeah, I don't know about it either. I know she deserves it, though."

"Yeah, she does."

"I think..." Jaime stopped and slowly dropped to his knees. He set the bags aside and frantically started trying to rub out the words, "I'm not finished" from the sidewalk.

Imani and Mary looked back. "What's wrong?" Imani asked. "What's he doing?"

Dito knelt down and put her arm around him. He's just had too much to drink, I think. He'll be okay. Let's just get him to the campsite."

"You okay, Jaimz?" Dito whispered in his ear. "Can you get up?"

"Can you lift him, Dito?" Mary asked.

"Yeah, I got him, Mary. I'll make sure he gets to the campsite safely. You go on ahead with the others."

Jaime dropped to his hands and knees and hung his head.

"What are you doing? What's the matter?"

"I'm trying to... why won't they leave me alone?"

"Let's sit back down for a minute. Come here."

They both sat down on the sidewalk and Dito took his hands.

"It doesn't matter, Jaime. It doesn't matter what you believe or what I believe. Or what anyone believes. It doesn't matter if this is the work of some god, or just mere coincidence. Look at me."

Jaime lifted his head.

"It doesn't matter. Okay?"

"You don't see the message, do you?" Jaime asked.

"What message?"

"What's the point of this?" He tore the cross from his neck and threw it across the road.

Dito jumped up and dodged a passing car to go after it. She picked it up out of the ditch and walked back towards Jaime and sat down. She reached over and placed it back around his neck.

"Your mother gave this to you to keep you safe Jaime, and someday you'll pass it along to someone else. Don't give up on it just because you can't figure it out. Mary's right, you're confused, but that's okay. It only means that you got your eyes open."

He stood up and began to pace.

"Let's go, Jaimz. Mary will want you there when she tells everyone her news. You can drink yourself into an unconscious sleep if you want, nobody will care, and we'll watch out for you."

"I need to go see my mother tomorrow."

"Wait, I thought..."

"Her gravesite."

"Oh, yeah, okay."

"She would've loved you."

"Yeah?"

"Yeah, you're such a good person."

Dito smiled and reached over and took his hand.

Monday and Briena reached the campsite before the rest. He collected what was left around the campfire and carried them to the stream. He needed to wash dishes. Briena watched him through her tears.

CHAPTER 19

There's This Girl Though

Lisa woke up with the sound of music in her head. She stretched and rubbed her eyes at the sunlight coming in through the window. Snuggled into Gwen's bed, she couldn't remember how or when she got there, but she had fallen asleep during last night's movie, and Gwen must have managed to lead her back into the bedroom.

She sat up, pulled her hair back from her face, kicked the covers off, and ran through the apartment, but Gwen wasn't there. She looked at the clock in the hallway, it was already past ten. "The library!" she thought. "I need to get my ticket!" Lisa ran into the bathroom, cleaned up as fast as she could, and started towards the door. She stopped, ran back again to look in the mirror, brushed her hair once more, and ran out.

Jaime parked in the shadow of the cathedral. A light snow had fallen the night before, leaving everyone at the campsite tucked into their tents for the morning. Sleep didn't come for him last night. He laid awake thinking about Lisa, remembering how it felt to hold her. It was cold, and sometime during the night, Bombay had rolled over and snuggled in. He smiled and pulled him in closer. It wasn't the same, but he felt an affection for Bombay, and the body heat was welcomed. He looked at his watch. The early morning light was streaming through the tent. He wanted nothing more than to sleep, but it was too late now.

Jaime carefully extracted himself from Bombay's embrace and quietly unzipped the tent door. He stretched, put his jacket on, and looked around at the snow-dusted tents. He moved through the rhododendron gathering up as many branches as he could. The snapping of wood breaking against his knee woke Dito. He heard the tent zipper and looked over to see her sleepy eyes peering out.

"Hey."

"Hey, Dito. Sorry, I didn't mean to wake you."

"It's okay. You're up early. You still going to see your mom today?" She whispered through a yawn.

"Yeah, but I thought I'd get the fire going first."

"Thanks, Jaimz. Some of us are going with Mary to help get her place ready to move into. Will you be back today?"

"Yeah, I'll be back. I gotta be at work by noon, so I'm trying to get an early start."

"Okay, I'll see you later. I hope you have a good visit."

Jaime folded his lips in and nodded his head.

"Thanks, Dito. Now go cover up. You hate the cold!"

"I do!" she said laughing.

"You're gonna leave soon, aren't you? I mean, you're gonna get back on the train and head South soon, aren't you?"

Dito was zipping up, but paused, unzipped, and looked out at Jaime. "We don't gotta talk about that now."

"Okay," he said. "Trains."

"What?" she whispered back.

"Trains."

"Jaime."

"I hate trains."

"I know you do. Now go see her. I'll come by the shop later and check on you."

"I hate trains," he said to himself, as Dito zipped up her tent.

It had been over a year since he'd visited his mother. Jaime turned the rearview mirror and looked into it, wanting to see her in himself, but he was never quite sure he did. Maybe her eyes. People used to tell him he had her heart, but you can't really see that. At least not in a mirror. He crushed his cigarette out and scanned the grounds ahead for wandering nuns.

He walked up the gravel path towards the cemetery that spread along and beyond the side of the church. The bench where he and Sister Anna had sat and talked years before always made him uneasy. It was more than the reminder of an awful day. He looked over with a bitter contempt and rushed it, shoving his hands against it to turn it over, but it was secured to the ground. His feet slid out from under him on the gravel and he landed onto it in a praying position. He surrendered, closed his eyes, and lowered his forehead onto his arms.

Lisa closed the door behind her and stepped out onto the sidewalk in front of Gwen's apartment. She looked both ways before crossing the road, and then quickly back to her left again where a police car was parked a block away. Her heart was in her throat. She slowly turned and started walking down the sidewalk in the opposite direction, when she heard car doors closing behind her. She slowly turned to see two policemen crossing the street. She pushed through the people on the sidewalk in front of her and took off running. Turning the corner, her feet nearly slid out from under her as she ducked behind a dumpster outside the parking garage entrance. She closed her eyes, held her breath, and pressed her head against her arms that were stretched across her knees. The two police officers ran past her and into the garage. She immediately darted out and ran back in the direction that she'd come. "I've gotta get to the library!" she thought. But the policemen saw her through the garage opening and were back in pursuit, chasing her down the sidewalk.

As she ran towards the intersection ahead, Lisa spotted a pickup truck in the line of cars that were waiting on the light. "Turn, turn, turn!" she pleaded. She looked back over her shoulder, Nona changed the thread in her loom from red to green, pulled it through, and the truck's tailpipes rattled as it took off. Lisa ran along its back corner, threw her backpack in, and climbed over the tailgate. The startled driver looked in his rearview mirror at Lisa, who was on her knees with her hands clasped at her chin in a begging position. The driver could see the police officers with hands on hips, trying to catch their breath at the corner behind them. He'd never liked the cops anyway, especially since they threw him in jail last year for an ounce of grass. He laughed at the defeated looks on their faces and motioned for Lisa to get down. "It's okay girl, I gotcha," he said into his mirror.

He turned the corner and sped down the highway towards the interstate. He needed to beat the cops to the truck stop. Lisa held onto the side, with the wind in her hair, and watched the library disappear from view.

"We have a more comfortable place in the church to pray young man," the sister said, resting her hand on his shoulder.

Jaime had fallen asleep and was startled by her touch. "What?" he asked, looking around.

"The church, you are more than welcome to come in and say your prayers where it's warm."

He had stiffened from the cold and was trying to stand up. Leaning over and holding on to the bench, he paused. "Thanks, sister, but I'm finished."

"Would you like some help?" she asked.

"No, I'm fine. I'm just gonna go over and visit my mother's gravesite," he said, as he finally managed the difficult climb to his feet.

"Well, Lord bless you, child."

Jaime tried to cross himself back at the nun but got it all terribly wrong. She watched as he appeared to be encircling an exclamation point across his body. She turned to hide her laughter and continued walking towards the church.

He took a deep breath, stiffened his arms, and shrugged his shoulders against the cold as he slid his hands into his pockets, and walked over towards his mother. "Here you are, momma, surrounded by all these people I don't even know or care about. You don't belong here," he said, as he looked around. "I wish I could take you up to a mountain and let you rest all on your own. You deserve better. You deserve a mountain."

However crowded with nefarious strangers this place might be, it was sacred to Jaime. Not because of the church, but because it held the body of the angel that used to hold his, through every moment of anger and despair. She would never put him off with answers, or try pacifying him with, "Everything will be alright." She knew him better than he knew himself. She would just hold him, run her fingers through his hair, and tell him she loved him. At nights, when she would hear him struggling, she'd run to him, sit on the side of his bed, and rub his chest, singing to him until he calmed. Her voice was rich and beautiful, and when she sang, the meadowlarks blushed.

She thought the sun rose and set on her boy. Bombay filled Jaime's head with thoughts the night before, but his mother filled his heart with a warmth and love that suspended all of his thoughts. And she always knew that's what he needed more than anything else-to get out of his head.

"I think your candle's burning out, momma," he said, as he sat next to her, "and I don't know what to do." He tried striking a match, but the wind kept blowing it out, and the coincidence was perfect. "You're not here to keep it lit anymore and, well, I got some good friends, you'd really like them, but I think I'm ready to just let it go out." He looked down at the ground between his legs, hesitated, and then turned to her. "There's this girl though, and I love her so much. But I don't know if she loves me, and it scares me to think that she might not. She's supposed to write me. If she did, I should get it today. But if she doesn't write I'll never know how to find her. I messed up. I shouldn't have let her go. I wish you could tell me what to do."

He pulled his collar up closer around his neck. "That demon's still after me," he said, looking over at the bench. "Those weren't just dreams I was having, but I guess you know that now. Can you see them at all? Can you tell them to stop? Can you tell them to leave me alone?" Jaime sat in silence, not really expecting an answer. "Your cross has kept me safe so far, but I don't know for how much longer. They want me to kill myself. I think that's what he was doing those nights I woke up scared. I think he was putting these feelings in my chest, my heart, and now, well, now I just don't know what to do. I guess I'll probably do it. I'm trying to do the best I can, though, and I want you to be proud of me, but I don't know what to do. I don't know what happens when people die. I don't know if you're here or not. Sometimes I think if I just do it, I'll be with you again."

Jaime looked down and fidgeted with the zipper of his jacket. "Momma, I remember arguing with you once about Janet. I don't know what it was about exactly, but it was after a school skating party. I must've thought that I had it all figured out, or whatever, I don't know. But I don't have anything figured out, and I know that now. I remember that night cause you grabbed me by my shoulders and told me that even though we were only children, we could still love, and that no matter how much I thought I knew about everything, love was the one problem I was never gonna solve. I remember that, and you were right. I don't understand love, and while nothing seems to have a reason, I think maybe love doesn't need a reason. Maybe love is its own reason. I don't know. I just know that Lisa warms my heart the way that you did, well, in a different way I guess, but you know what I mean. That's her name, Lisa. And I miss her so much."

"I've gotta get out of this town, and I need to get back to Tennessee. I haven't done anything wrong. I don't know why they're after me."

"I wish I could help you, but they'll be looking for my truck now, so I'd better get going or I'll lead them right to you."

"Yeah, I suppose you'd better get going. Thanks for your help. I'll hide out here until I can figure something out."

"Here, take this and get you something to eat. Ask around inside. Surely one of these truckers are heading that way. I know it's kinda scary, but I'm not sure what else to tell you."

"It wouldn't be the first time I've hitched a ride. You don't have to do this," she said, handing him back his money.

"Take it. It's only ten bucks. Seriously, I gotta go. They'll be coming down this road after us any minute now."

He circled his truck around, and as he pulled out, he rolled his window down, "Good luck! uh…"

"It's Lisa, my name's Lisa!"

He raced out of the parking lot just as the police were coming into view. She watched as they followed him down the highway and then she ran inside.

"Can I help you?" the woman behind the counter asked.

"I don't know," she said frantically. "I need to get to Tennessee!"

"Well, I'm headin' that way. I'd be glad to give you a ride."

Lisa looked over at the man lifting the front of his cowboy hat to her. She looked back at the woman behind the counter who shook her head, "no." Lisa felt uneasy about it. "I don't have a choice though," she thought to herself. "When are you leaving?" she asked.

"Lemme pay for my fuel, and we can git goin'."

"Which one's yours?"

"Huh?"

"Which truck? Which truck's yours?"

"The red one over there."

"Is it unlocked?"

"Huh?"

"Is it unlocked!" Lisa didn't have time for his stuttering.

"Yeah, I think so."

Lisa ran out the back door as the police were pulling into the front lot. She climbed into the truck and watched out the window.

CHAPTER 20

Wichita, 4 Miles

It was late afternoon when the crew gathered back around the campsite.

"Thanks, y'all for helping," Mary said.

Rookie picked up the stick he'd use to stir the fire and began digging around to see if there were any embers left from the morning. "You're welcome, Mary. I'm glad you're finally gettin' outta here."

"Just in time, too!" Carol added. "Jasmine said it's gonna get cold and rainy the next few days."

Dito wrapped her arms around her legs, pulled her knees into her chest, stared into the firepit, and thought about the train. She hated the cold.

Rookie found nothing. He never did, but everyone has their rituals. "Yeah, she says it's sposed to get below freezing tomorrow night and then turn to rain on Wednesday."

Dito unzipped her tent and curled up into her sleeping bag.

"Hey, Dito. Aren't you gonna eat?"

"No, I'm not really hungry. I'm gonna read for a bit and then probably go on to sleep."

"Okay, well I'm gonna heat up some beans and make a pot of chili if you change your mind."

"Thanks, Carol," Dito said, from inside her closed tent.

"Answered prayers," Imani whispered into Mary's ear, as she hugged her tight. "Heaven's right around the corner."

"He's faithful," Mary replied. "It's like the preacher said, all I gotta do is trust him."

"I don't understand why they can't just let you in tonight though," Monday said. "I mean, it's only two days."

"Rules are rules, Monday. I'm sure I'll survive for two more days."

"Get off me!" Lisa kicked at him. The rope burned her wrists as she pulled and fought.

"Hold still, I said!"

For a split second, she saw Raymond's face in his. "You're not taking this away from me, Raymond!" she screamed. Nona swept in through the air vents, held his head in place, and with all of her strength, Lisa landed the heel of her foot into his bearded jaw. It was over. The truckdriver's eyes rolled back into his head, and Lisa watched evil slump into unconsciousness against the door. Knowing that he could come to at any moment, she grabbed him by his long red hair, slammed his face against the window once more, and then opened the door with her tied hands. She climbed down from the truck and took off running into the woods that separated the rest stop from the interstate.

"I don't know where you are Nona, but I'm going back to Jaime with or without your help."

Nona smiled from within the wind. "I haven't forgotten you, sweetheart. There are forces that are trying to undo, and I'm traveling the world as fast as I can. You have a special place in my heart. Keep running. You'll find Sandra, who's returning to Oklahoma City, at the gas station. She doesn't know how she's lost her keys, but you'll get there before she finds them."

Lisa saw lights beyond the trees and ran towards them. The woods finally broke open to an isolated area with a small gas station just off the interstate. She stopped to catch her breath, and looking to her left, she saw a sign that read, "Wichita 4 miles." She dropped to her knees and exhaled. "I'm further from Tennessee than I was when I started!" She crawled over and sat with her back against a small tree, resisted the impulse to give up, and using her teeth, she began pulling the knots out of the rope. A car pulled into the gas station and Lisa looked up and across the street. She saw a woman get out and walk into the store. Lisa pulled harder on the rope. Night would be falling soon.

Jaime walked to his car and pulled a blanket out from the back seat. He was tired and making it back for work wasn't likely to happen. He closed the door and decided that he wasn't even gonna try. He wrapped the blanket around him and curled up over his mother's grave. It was cold and overcast. He pulled the blanket over his head and curled up tighter. "Are you in heaven, momma?" Restless, he rolled over onto his other side. "Cause I don't understand it. I don't believe in god, and even if he's real, he doesn't care. I mean, my friends are living in the woods. But then there's Mary, she's my friend too, and she's finally getting a home. Is it because of god? She believes it is. Or is it just random luck? I wish you could say something. I wish you could talk to me."

He tried shifting again and getting comfortable on the hard ground. "I'm probably gonna try and take a nap. I'm really tired. I miss you. I wish you could sing to me again." Jaime closed his eyes, but then slowly moved the blanket from his face to see the small bird perched and singing on the statue of Mary which stood in the center of the graveyard. He pulled it back further and felt the embrace of a warm gentle wind filling his blanket as the bird flew towards him and landed on his mother's headstone, just above him. It began singing again, only this time softer. Jaime turned over, wrapped the warmth up in his blanket, and closed his eyes.

Gwen came home for lunch only to find Lisa, and all of her belongings, gone. Her bus was scheduled to leave at one. She collapsed into the armchair next to her bookcase and wondered where Lisa could be, and why she'd left without coming by the library. "Something's wrong." Gwen could think of only one explanation. She took her glasses off and buried her face in her hands before walking back to the bedroom to check for a note. The blankets were left thrown aside, but there was no note. She looked around the room one last time and then left for the police station.

"Excuse me," Lisa called out, as she crossed the street and approached the gas pumps.

The woman looked up and over at her. "Yes?"

Lisa stepped towards her and asked, "I need to get to Oklahoma City. Is there any chance you're going that way, and could I please, please, please get a ride with you, if you are? I'm stranded here and it's gonna get dark soon, and I'm scared. I only have a few dollars, but I'll give it to you."

"I *am* going to Oklahoma City dear, and I'll be glad to give you a ride. And you don't have to give me a dime. It's just that I've lost my car keys. I can't find them anywhere."

"Is that them?" Lisa asked.

"Where?"

"In the ignition."

Sandra looked inside, and there they were. She laughed, both in relief that she'd found them, and at herself for looking everywhere but there. "I can't believe this..."

"Lisa, my name's Lisa."

"Lisa! My name's Sandra. Here, can I take your pack for you and put it in the back seat? Do you need anything out of it?"

"No, I don't. Thank you, Sandra." She pulled it off her shoulder and handed it to her.

Sandra had the kindest eyes, but they could turn angry when things were wrong, and they were, and they did. She tried to hide her expression, but it was hard seeing the state Lisa was in, and what she was sure were rope burns on Lisa's wrists. She slowly placed the pack in the back seat while trying to take in what she was seeing. She looked over at Lisa who was standing on the other side of the car trying to discreetly massage her wrists. She looked weak.

"Are you hungry, Lisa? I can get you some food from the store?"

"Thank you, but I'm okay. You don't have to do that. I'm just so grateful for you giving me a ride." Lisa looked over and down the road. The truck was slowly turning out of the side street and would soon be heading her way.

"Sandra, may I go ahead and get in your car?" she asked nervously.

Sandra followed Lisa's eyes down the road and back. "Get inside, Lisa. Hurry! Close the door and slide down into the seat. You're safe now."

Sandra got in and turned the key and watched as the truck slowly drove past the gas station. She pulled out and came to a stop behind him at the traffic light. Her eyes were locked on the chain wrapped around the latch. "Why does he need a chain?" she inadvertently asked out loud.

"What?" Lisa asked.

"Oh, nothing, I was just..."

Lisa raised up, looked at the chain, and then over at Sandra who was trying hard not to let her fears spill out. Sandra ran the license plate numbers over and over in her head until she had them memorized. The light changed, and the truck pulled off.

"Hey, you know what? I think I'm gonna run back into that store and get a few snacks and drinks for the drive. Is that okay with you?"

Lisa's eyes remained far away. "Sure."

They were both fixated on what was behind those doors. Maybe nothing. Maybe discarded souls. Maybe screams of "help." Maybe nothing.

Sandra parked the car and went inside.

"Excuse me, can I use your phone?"

The young man behind the counter looked up. "All we got is that payphone over there."

"That's fine. Can you give me change for a dollar?"

Lisa got on her knees and reached into the back seat and into her pack for a sweater. She dug around and pulled it out, and with it fell a book onto the floor. "What?" She climbed over the front seat and picked it up. She sat down and slowly placed it in her lap with both hands. It was the book from her childhood, *The Three Sisters*. She turned through the pages and found "Oklahoma City Library" stamped on the back cover. "Gwen," she said. "But how? How did she know?" She held the book against her chest and curled up in the back seat.

Sandra hurried through the pages of the phonebook and found the number for the Wichita police department. She gave them the license plate numbers and a description of the truck. She told them she thought she'd seen the driver loading drugs into the back, and that they'd probably want to open it up and look around.

"Thank you for the tip, ma'am," said the woman on the other end of the line. "We have an officer in your vicinity and he's on his way right now."

"Thank you. I'm really concerned about what he may have in the back of his truck."

"We'll look into it," she said.

Sandra hung the phone up and walked back out to the car.

"They didn't have what you wanted?" Lisa asked.

"What?"

"The snacks and drinks you went back for. They didn't have what you wanted?"

"Lisa, why are you in the back seat?"

"I needed a sweater and couldn't reach it."

Sandra put her key into the ignition and stared into the dashboard.

"Lisa, did he hurt you?"

Lisa turned away and looked out the window. "No. He was trying to, but I got away."

Sandra closed her eyes and rested her forehead on the steering wheel. "But what if you hadn't?"

Lisa looked down at her wrists.

"I don't know, Sandra."

"Do you have a safe place to go?"

"I do if I can ever get there. I just need to get back to Oklahoma City first."

"Well, we'll be there in about two and a half hours. Why don't you come back up front with me."

Lisa put her sweater on and started to climb back over into the front seat.

"Maybe you should use the doors," Sandra said with a gentle laugh.

"Oh, yeah. Okay. And do you mind if I read my book while you drive?"

"No, not at all. What's it about?"

Lisa closed the door and locked it. "Oh, it's just a silly fairy tale about these three sisters who try and turn sad and scared people's lives into happy and safe ones."

It was late afternoon when Jaime woke up. He looked at his watch, said a painful goodbye to his mother, walked past the bench and back to his car. He needed to get home and find out if Lisa had written him.

Mary said her evening prayers.

The city police were given their directives. They were to clear it out in the morning.

CHAPTER 21

Sleeping Beauty, Don

Chief Dodson yawned, finished her coffee, and began sorting through the work piled on her desk.

"How are your guys set for clearing out the homeless camp in the morning?" she asked without looking up.

"They're ready to go. The clear out is never the problem, you know that. It's chasing them all over town and through the woods afterwards," Captain Thomas answered. "That's the problem."

"Yeah, well, it's gotta be done. I'm tired of the complaints. And no one ever said you had to chase them. Just do what you've sworn to do Don, protect and serve. I'll be glad to tell you when and when not to chase folks. And I'm about to do just that."

He stood up and adjusted his belt.

"The complaints won't stop just 'cause we run 'em off, Chief. I've said it before, the way things are now, we at least know where most of 'em are at night when we need to throw 'em in jail. Look, I hate the homeless as much as you, but…"

"Don't finish that sentence, Don. Just because you work for me doesn't mean you know me. You don't know me. I don't hate those folks."

She stared him back down into the chair across from her desk, pulled Lisa's diary out of her top drawer, and started turning through the pages.

"Listen, we're dropping the Gillis investigation. I've already talked it over with…"

"Just like that!"

"…Carter at the DA's office and he agrees. So you can stop chasing that one."

Captain Thomas folded his arms across his chest. "Why?"

"First of all, Don, we've got nothing on Felts or Harris. Nothing. And I don't think we're gonna get a confession by bluffing our way through it. Well, I don't know about Harris, but I know damn well we're not gonna get one out of Felts. And maybe 'dropping' isn't exactly the right word, but we're certainly suspending it. We have plenty of other cases we need to work on that we may actually get somewhere with."

"But…"

"But nothing, listen. I've been going through this diary and I've concluded two things. First, I think it's obvious that Harris was falling in love with Felts, and that one or both of them did it. But like I said, we have nothing on them, well, except that tire, and there's no way of connecting it with Felts' car. And second…"

"But…"

"Shut up! And second, Gillis was an absolute monster. I've read through these pages. He was a slow killer, and I think you know it. My god, Don, if Harris *were* ever charged, this diary could probably show cause for self-defense. This was his fate. The world's better off without him. And I'm not gonna play the role of Maleficent for you."

Captain Thomas looked confused.

"Sleeping Beauty, Don."

She waited. "I'm not bringing someone to ruin over your grudge for them."

"So..."

"So, let me finish. None of what I said excuses it, or makes anything about this okay, but I'm not pursuing it anymore. And neither are you. If anything surfaces... "

Captain Thomas raised his eyebrow.

"I know, I know. If anything," she paused to find the words, "comes to light, then okay, but otherwise call it off. I'm gonna contact Oklahoma City and tell them we've suspended the investigation and that they can stop wasting their time trying to catch Harris, if that's even where she is."

She tilted her head to the side. "And please don't suddenly get righteous with me, like you really care about bringing justice to Gillis. You had him in and out of that jail," she said with her arm outstretched and pointing, "constantly. He's been causing all kinds of trouble across town. I see through you Don, and I know what this is all about. You couldn't intimidate Felts, and he laughed at you. You just want to settle that score. You want to show him who's boss. Well, I'm the boss Don, like it or not, and the chase is off."

Captain Thomas slowly stood up.

"You ever kept a diary?"

"Do I look like…"

"There's no such thing as a "look like" Don. Jesus Christ, you men are exhausting."

She ran her hands through her hair and leaned back to re-gather herself.

"So, I'll tell you. To the owner, they're sacred. I want this returned to Harris' home and put right back in the place where it was found, if possible."

She handed him the diary.

He mumbled something under his breath and turned to walk out of the office.

"I meant what I said, Don."

He slammed the door behind him, crashing the blinds into the glass pane.

Chief Dodson rose up from her chair and stumbled as she hurried out from behind her desk after him. She opened the door only to see Captain Thomas storming and stomping down the hallway. She started to call out to him but was struck by the sight of an old woman smiling and knitting in one of the metal chairs by the desk across from her door. She curiously studied her for a second.

"Is someone helping you ma'am?" she asked.

"Is someone helping *me*?" she replied with a suppressed laugh. "Oh, I don't need any help dear, thank you though. I just needed to make sure this one thread was in place. I'm calling it the sword of truth."

Chief Dodson narrowed her eyes at the woman. "How did you know…" The woman raised her eyebrows. Chief Dodson looked over at her office. "How the hell did she know that I just made a *Sleeping Beauty* reference?" she thought. "The door was closed." Not knowing what she meant, or how to reply, she walked over to one of the booking officers to ask about the woman, but when she turned to point her out, she was gone.

Sandra turned the corner and Lisa sighed with relief at seeing the library.

"That's it," she said. "Just down there on the right." Lisa nervously scanned the streets around her.

"I don't see the police anywhere. I think you're safe to run inside."

"Neither do I, but what if Gwen's not there? I mean, it's late, and then I'll have to try and get to her place without getting caught. And what if she's not there either?"

"Don't worry, I'm not gonna leave you, Lisa. Run inside and check. If she's not there, come back out and I'll take you over to her place. And if she's not there, my offer is still good."

"Okay, thanks, Sandra."

Lisa looked around once more, got out of the car, and then ran up the steps and into the library.

"Excuse me, Is Gwen here? I mean Mrs., umm… "

"Mrs. Conner? And please Lisa, shhhh."

"Yes! Mrs. Conner! Oh, sorry. Yes, Mrs. Conner," Lisa repeated in a whispered voice.

"No, she left over an hour ago. Can I help you?" asked Simon.

"No thanks!" Lisa shouted back as she ran towards the door. She stopped and looked back. "It's Simon, right?"

Simon nodded his head and laughed. "Yeah, now go, you loudmouth!"

Sandra reached over and opened the door for her.

"She's not there. Can you take me to her place?"

"Sure, just give me directions," Sandra looked into her mirror, "Wait! Get down!"

Lisa laid over onto Sandra's lap and waited until the police car slowly passed.

"It's okay now. You can get up."

Lisa raised her head, and they both watched as it continued down the street, and finally out of view.

"Gosh Lisa, I wish you could find out why they're after you. I'm sure it's like you said, that your boyfriend has something to do with it, but... "

"Sandra, please don't call him my boyfriend."

"Oh, I'm sorry Lisa. "

"It's okay."

"But I'm still worried this isn't gonna end when you get back to Tennessee."

"*If* I get back to Tennessee," Lisa said, as she stared out the window.

Sandra started the car. "You'll get back there. It's your fate," she said with a smile. "What's her name again?"

"Nona."

"Yeah, Nona. You've got me believing in her too. Listen, you have an incredible story Lisa, and that's just from what you've told me along the journey. And I can tell you're strong, but no one's this lucky - to have survived all that you have without some help."

Lisa looked over at her.

"Well, she can stop waiting 'til the last second." She pulled the book out of her bag and held it up to her face, "You hear me, Nona! If you're out there, my heart can't take much more of this. Please! Just get me on that bus."

Sandra gently pulled the book from Lisa's hands with a sympathetic smile and placed it back in her pack. "I'm sure she's listening dear, now where to?"

Just over there, from the window, was where Lisa had called him in from the rain that morning. Jaime remembered the light in her eyes, and the image flooded his soul. He pulled on the handbrake and stared off towards the small market that sat across a vacant lot, behind his house. He watched as the listless figures walked in and out.

"Absurd bridges we cross from need to need."

He pulled out a cigarette and reached under his seat.

"There's no sustenance to be found."

He twisted the cap off, rolled the window down, and started drinking.

"We chase moments, that's all. Moments of sensory distraction from the meaninglessness of it all."

He looked back at the window. But Lisa.

The thought of a letter broke his stare. He got out of the car and tried to temper his expectation of finding one. He rounded the corner of the house, stepped onto the front porch, and approached the letterbox by the door. There was nothing. He walked over and sat down on the steps and hung his head. "How could I have been such a goddammed fool." He lifted his tear-soaked eyes to see the young girl on her bike again, riding by and laughing at him. She turned and began riding in circles in front of his house, taunting him with her bell. He dropped his head and tried to rub the vision out of his eyes.

"She never loved you!" she said, throwing her head back and laughing. "Maybe you should kill yourself!"

Jaime wiped his eyes and looked up to see Ezra riding on her handlebars, both of them laughing. As they turned and began riding away, he could see the demon's tail from outside the back of the young girl's dress. He looked around to see if anyone was watching. The street was empty, apart from two children drawing their pictures with sidewalk chalk. Jaime envied their innocence.

He stood up and walked around to the back door that opened into the kitchen. He slowly closed it behind him as his eyes became fixed on the silverware drawer. He set the bottle down on the counter and went back to the bedroom closet where he kept a small tool chest. He removed the tray and dug through it until he found the box cutter. He pushed the razor up to see its edge, then retracted the blade and sat down on the side of the bed.

He patted the box cutter into the palm of his hand and thought about these visions, the demon, his mother, the cross, Mary... He stood up and began pacing the room. "What if?" He walked into the kitchen and grabbed the vodka from the counter to fire his imagination. "What if?" He thought about his mother's prayers of protection, and her singing to him through the bird. He thought about Mary and her prayers for a house, and its coming true for her. Maybe not the one in her dreams, but still.

He sat down on the floor against the wall and lit a cigarette. "I mean, Dito's right, it doesn't matter if it's the work of some god or just coincidence, luck, whatever. But what if?"

He looked at the wall that separated his side of the duplex from Lisa's and wondered about good and evil, what separates a monster from a saint? Are these forces real, or are they just mad hallucinations? "They seem real to me, and what if they are? Couldn't there be good forces at work too?"

So he did what most people do during times of fear and desperation-he set aside reason in exchange for a supernatural chance.

He rolled over onto his knees, crushed his cigarette out, and felt for the cross around his neck. Jaime hadn't uttered a prayer since his mother died and screaming at god probably didn't count as a prayer. This was not going to be easy. He closed his eyes, dispatched his soul, and prayed to this god, that Mary believed gave her a home. He asked him, or her, or whomever, to bring Lisa back.

Sandra pulled the car over and Lisa looked up at the window into Gwen's apartment.

"Well, I guess I'll go in and see if she's home."

Lisa and Sandra both looked around the area, and with no police in sight, Lisa got out. She turned back and opened the door. "Is it alright if I leave my backpack in here?"

"Of course it is, but I got a good feeling. I think she's gonna be there."

"I hope so," Lisa said, crossing her fingers. She looked up and down the street one last time and then hurried in through the front door. She climbed the stairs to the third floor, took a deep breath and pressed the buzzer. The door opened as far as the chain would allow, and Gwen peered out.

"Hi, Gwen."

Gwen closed the door to unchain it, and then flung it open wide.

"Lisa!"

Gwen threw her arms open and Lisa rushed into her embrace.

"I've been worried sick about you, sweetheart. What happened? Where did you go?"

"I'm so sorry, Gwen. I'll tell you all about it. But could I stay with you for at least tonight? I don't have anywhere to go. You don't have to buy me another ticket. I'll find a way back."

Gwen placed her finger over Lisa's mouth. "You're staying right here for as long as you need to, and, yes, I am gonna get you a ticket sweetheart. Where's your bag?"

"It's downstairs. I'll run and get it. A really nice woman gave me a ride back and it's in her car. I need to tell her goodbye, too."

"A ride back from where?"

"Wichita."

"What!"

"I'll tell you about it when I get back." Lisa started off, but then stepped back into Gwen's arms. "It's good to see you, Gwen."

"It's good to see you too, Lisa. I'm so glad you're here and safe. Now run down and get your bag. We have some catching up to do. And we'll figure out supper and a movie and everything!"

"Okay!" Lisa squeezed her tight and then ran back down the stairs to Sandra.

"She's here!" Lisa said, as she opened the car door and sat down. Thank you for everything, Sandra. I feel like you saved my life."

"Oh, you're welcome Lisa. I'm just glad I *happened* to be there. Sandra winked. Just think of me as another thread woven into your life story."

Sandra leaned over and whispered in Lisa's ear, "Keep your head up, love. She's not finished!"

CHAPTER 22

This Stream, This Joining of Waters

Jaime woke before the sun Tuesday morning. Holding Lisa's pillow against him, he stared at the ceiling. With an eye on the missing tile, he summoned every argument he could against this god whom he had prayed to the night before. This god whom Mary believed had delivered her from the woods and had given her a home.

These arguments were never resolved in his mind. "Why deliver this one, but not that one, or why that one, and not this one? How can I possibly make sense of any of this? I've seen monsters swimming in wealth and pleasure, while saints are drowning in pain and poverty. Is he, she, they, whatever, watching with as much curiosity as to how things will turn out for each of us as we are?" He reached over and tapped his cigarette on the ashtray. "There could be a god," he posited, "but if so, his decisions are as erratic as a two-year-old's. Maybe he's just in over his head."

We think of this god as loving towards all his creation, but Jaime had completely dismissed that Christian narrative years ago. If one was to reconcile a god with this reality on earth, then you have no choice but to accept that he's capricious and petty, and the best you can do is to send him your appeals and hope he gives a damn. It's not exactly Aladdin's lamp, but probably not far from it.

His room stood quiet. He took the cross in his hand and drifted into a paralysis of thought. "Maybe I should ask Mary to pray for me." The door of hope swung open like a curtain by the sequined game show hostess. But before he walked through to claim his eternal prize, he decided to spend some time alone, grounded on the planet. He climbed out of bed, lit another cigarette, pulled his backpack from the closet, and began making plans for a night in the mountains.

"Do y'all have any room for me?" she called out as she approached the campsite.

"Who are you? Come closer, we can't see you," Imani called back.

Everyone had gone to bed except Imani and Mary. They were still up talking over Mary's plans for her big move on Wednesday.

She came closer.

"My name's Grace. I just got kicked out of the mission and don't have anywhere to sleep tonight. This guy told me about y'all's camp down here, so I thought I'd ask if you had any room for me."

She continued into the light of the fire.

"Child, you're pregnant!" Mary said.

"Yes ma'am, I am. Would y'all have any space for me? I don't have any money to give you, but I'll just stay the night and figure things out in the morning. I'm so tired ."

"Of course we do!" Imani said.

Mary stood up and took her by the hand and led her to a seat on the log. "You'll sleep in my tent tonight. I've got plenty of bedding and blankets."

Grace slowly sat down with Mary's help.

"Can I ask why they threw you out?"

"Well, I just wanted to take a shower and read my book, and I'd left it upstairs in the women's dorm, so I went back up to get it. A staff member shouted at me 'cause I wasn't supposed to be up there yet, and I shouted back at him. I was tired. I didn't mean to shout. I know I was wrong, but they just don't know what it's like to be tired and scared. I didn't mean to be short-tempered."

"No, they don't!" Imani said.

"Well, he grabbed my arm and pulled me into the chapel, wrestled me down to the floor, and yelled over for the woman at the desk to call the police."

Mary hung her head. "Those people. May the lord have mercy on their souls."

"Four policemen came in and handcuffed me. One of them pressed his knee into my back to hold me on the floor. I told them I was pregnant, and he told me to shut up, and that I could either leave peacefully or be taken to jail."

Imani stood and walked over to sit on Grace's other side. She took her one hand and Mary took the other.

Mary reached over. "Do you mind?"

"No, I don't mind."

Mary placed her hand on Grace and smiled. "She's kicking."

"I know, and I hope she's a she," Grace said, "but I don't know yet, I don't have the money to go to a doctor."

"Don't you have family Grace?" Imani asked.

"They won't have anything to do with me. I didn't mean to get pregnant, but he said..."

"We know," Imani stopped her, with Mary nodding in agreement, "you don't even need to finish that sentence. And lemme guess, he's outta sight now?"

"Yeah," Grace said with a yawn.

Mary squeezed her hand. "Let's get you and that precious baby inside the tent. You need to sleep, girl. You're safe tonight."

"Get in here!" Gwen said, as Lisa reached the top of the stairs, "Wichita?"

Lisa came through and Gwen closed the door behind her. "Yeah."

Gwen could sense trauma and fatigue in her eyes and in her voice. She reached to take her backpack and noticed the marks on her wrists.

"Lisa."

"Yes, Gwen?"

"You don't have to talk about it, but you're safe tonight. Take your shoes off and curl up right here on the sofa. I'm gonna heat up some soup."

"Gwen."

"Yes?"

"I saw the book."

Gwen stopped short of the kitchen.

"I'm sorry, Lisa. I intended for you to find it on your bus ride back to Tennessee. I thought it might comfort you, whether true or not, like it always had me."

"What do you mean? And how did you know?"

"It's a book my mother used to read to me when I was young, just before bedtime. I remember falling asleep to the thoughts of someone arranging the whole universe to make me happy and safe. I don't know, it's like believing in a god though, right? But if it's true, then why did Nona let my Bobby kill himself? If god exists, then why does he let good things happen to some, and bad things happen to others?"

Lisa listened.

"I think maybe it's been this way forever. We cling to the chance of some supernatural white-bearded man in times of despair because there doesn't seem to be any answers lying around here. We finally give up and place our bets on some disembodied paradise somewhere beyond the horizon."

Lisa glazed over all of that and then looked down at the shirt she'd been wearing for days.

"My life's been too crowded with pain and fear to think about these things Gwen, but Jaime is my horizon, and whatever I believe or don't believe about any of these things, well, I don't know, maybe I'll think about them someday. I've never, ever been in love until now, and it feels like being in a nest. And that's where I want to be, regardless of whatever I might or might not believe about Nona, god, or whatever. I'm tired of trying to figure it all out, Gwen. I just wanna get on that bus."

Gwen leaned against the threshold to the kitchen and crossed her arms. "I'm sorry Lisa, I know. It's a storm. Let's have some soup, cuddle up to a movie and try and take our minds off of it."

"It's okay, Gwen. The book brought back a lot of sweet and comforting memories. But I think I'm done with comfort. I'm on a mission."

Gwen smiled, and rocked herself off the doorframe, and went into the kitchen.

Jaime pulled into the parking space behind the shop and waited for Jasmine. It was early. He got out of his car, lit a cigarette, and sat down on the steps to the back door. His thoughts wandered back to the randomness of it all as he watched the moths fluttering around the lamp above him. A train rushing by startled him out of a near drift into sleep. He looked at his watch. Jasmine was still over an hour away from opening up, so he went back to his car and wrote a note on a paper bag.

"Jasmine, I won't be in today. I need some time in the mountains. You can tell Cyril whatever you want. I'll be back tomorrow, Jaime."

He rolled it up and placed it through the handle of the back door to the shop and left.

Gwen left a note on the bedside table for Lisa. "I'm off to the library, when you wake up, come and see me. Help yourself to breakfast and coffee."

They came in, and he grabbed the coffee pot from beside the fire ring and started banging his baton against it. "Alright everybody, wake up!"

One by one, tent doors were unzipping, and tired eyes were peering through.

"Time to clear out of here!" Captain Thomas shouted, as a squad of officers made their way through the campsite shaking tents.

Carol was the first to crawl out. She knew the drill from times before.

"Where can we go?"

"I don't care where you go, just get out of sight. And stay out of sight!"

Everyone else began slowly coming out of their tents, trying to adjust their eyes to the morning light, and their minds to what was going down.

"You mean we have to leave?" Rookie asked.

"Yes, what part of 'clear out' did you not understand?"

"But respected sir, we are only living. What could be the harm in that?" Bombay asked.

The officers encircling the group laughed.

"What's so goddammed funny!" Dito shouted at them, "You pigs..."

Imani reached over and put her arm around Dito, and whispered in her ear, "I can't go to jail again, Dito. I'm trying to get out of this mess, and every trip to jail makes it that much harder."

Dito closed her eyes and clenched her teeth. "I know Imani, I'm just so..."

"We'll be okay, Dito. We'll find another place. I love you for caring so much, but we're used to it."

"You shouldn't be," Dito replied under her breath, "this is wrong."

"How long do we have?" asked Mary.

"Sundown," said Captain Thomas. "We'll be back around six tonight, and any one of you who are still here will go to jail."

"For what! For existing!" Dito shouted back at him.

The closest officer to Dito started reaching for his handcuffs.

"You want to be the first?" Captain Thomas asked.

"Not gonna give you the pleasure, you fascist..."

"Dito! Please!"

"Sorry, Imani," she replied, as she threw her cigarette down and returned to her tent.

The officers looked over at Captain Thomas for directions. He shook his head and motioned for them to follow him out. "Anything left here will be taken to the dump," he said as they made their way back towards the hill.

Everyone stood still, looking at one another with the familiar feeling of, "what now?"

"I'll get a fire going," Rookie said, breaking the silence.

"I'll put some coffee on," Briena said.

"God's got a plan y'all," Mary called out as she walked back towards her tent, "just trust him."

Dito was on her hands and knees gathering all of her clothes and books. She loved and respected Mary, but dropped and shook her head at the notion that god had some plan for them all. She'd be on a train heading south soon, but what about these others? Her friends? Dito had said to Jaime once that she wasn't homeless, she was "home free." It was her choice to be a traveler, and if and when she were ever done with it, she could probably merge into the mainstream with some ease. She had a degree of privilege that she was aware of, but those outside her tent, trying to figure out where they would sleep tonight, had been pushed far beyond the margins, through no choice nor fault of their own.

The stream by the campsite was cascading over the rocks. Briena dipped the damaged coffee pot into the usual pool to fill it with water, as everyone began the work of taking down their tents. This place was sacred to her. It's where Monday goes to try and wash away his guilt.

Jaime returned to the fire ring and filled the metal filter with coffee and thought about Lisa. She said his coffee was too strong. That made him smile. He began the work of setting up his tent.

Tents were coming down as everyone discussed where they'd go for the night, and where they might find another place to set up camp.

Lisa finished her coffee and stepped outside, watching for the police as she made her way to the library.

CHAPTER 23

Where Can We Go

Jaime left his campsite and hiked along the trail, following the stream that ended in the pool where the two prongs converged. He crossed the smaller of the two and sat between them with his back against a tree. He remembered Bombay's words: *"I've seen two small, lonely mountain streams converge into one, and its fullness springs life. The waters from each become one, and they offer a place for happy fish to flourish. This stream, this joining of waters, it doesn't have to go anywhere..."*

He stared at the distant ridge to the sound of water cascading over rocks. The brook trout were asleep in the deep pool before him. "But the stream *does* go somewhere," he thought, "beyond what this pool can hold, it goes somewhere."

The two prongs drained the hollows and formed the stream that descended alongside the trail that led to Jaime's campsite. Where it ends, he didn't know. "And maybe that's not the point," he thought. "It's beautiful, it's peaceful, and the sound of it's comforting, like Lisa singing. Maybe Bombay's right. Or maybe he's not. I mean, it obviously goes somewhere, but what does it matter? What difference does anything make beyond this pool, this here, this now?" Jaime never really felt happiness, but he could recognize contentment, and he'd found it here, at this pool, in the shade of this tree. It seemed absurd to worry about where a stream ends when one doesn't have to follow it.

He pulled the bottle out of his jacket pocket and lit a cigarette. It wouldn't be long before the stream would calm his soul and repair the havoc the dishwasher had wreaked upon him. He knew as soon as he drove back into town, the demons that were determined to kill him would return to work. But if this peace could just stay with him for one night, maybe... he dismissed the thought before he'd even finished it.

Lisa stepped into the library and went up to the front desk. "I'm supposed to meet Gwen here."

Simon smiled, "Gwen?"

"Oh, I'm sorry, Mrs. Conner."

"It's okay, I call her Gwen, too. She'll be back soon. She ran over to the bus station.

Lisa closed her eyes and placed her hand on her heart. "Okay, I'll just look around while I wait."

"I'll probably go into town and hustle up enough for a room tonight. I can't do this cold," Dito said as she lit a cigarette and added wood to the fire, "anyone with me?"

"No thanks," said Rookie. "They don't know you like they know us. This is a small town and most of these people won't give us any money. They'll just offer to buy us a sandwich or something."

"Yeah, and if you ask again, they'll call the cops on you," Monday added.

The others nodded in agreement. "It's hard anymore," Carol said, "unless you go up to the intersections or exit ramps, and even then, you'll probably get run off or picked up."

"They think if they give you money, you're gonna buy drugs or alcohol with it," Imani said.

Without looking up from angrily stuffing her clothes in a bag, Carol shouted back, "And what if we do!"

"Exactly!" Imani said. "What if we do. We're not doing anything that they're not doing. I guess doing it in a house somehow makes it acceptable?"

"I wonder how they would cope with life out here?" Carol answered. "But I guess they got their home bars and prescription drugs."

Dito closed her eyes and shook her head, took a deep breath, and asked, "That's real, but what are y'all gonna do tonight? It's gonna be freezing!"

Carol looked up. "Me and Rookie are gonna head over to the garage off Seventeenth, and then figure it out."

"I'll be going with you," Bombay said, as he pulled tent stakes out from the ground. The sides of his tent began to collapse. He turned and rested on his knee, "Of course, the floor there is much harder than the ground here, but it's just across the street from the bus station, and the people passing by seem to be happy to give. I've stayed there many times in the past. Sometimes it's nice to sleep to the sound of people all around you."

A few others agreed, that if they could, they'd prefer to stay in the Seventeenth Avenue garage, or another like it. At least until this frigid night passes. Then they could start thinking about a new campsite.

Gwen came through the front door and saw Lisa across the open area, turning through a book. Lisa looked over, and Gwen waived a bus ticket with a smile. Lisa smiled back, slid the book back onto the shelf, and walked towards her. But as she approached the counter, the front door swung open, and two police officers entered. Lisa hurriedly walked past Gwen, her heart pounding in her chest. She hid behind the door in the hallway that led to a back exit. She thought about running.

"There's no need to run or hide anymore, Miss Harris. The warrant's been dropped," one of the officers called out.

Lisa looked out from behind the door. "Warrant?" she asked, as she slowly stepped out, and wrapped her arms around Gwen's waist from behind.

"You were wanted back in the state of Tennessee in regards to the death of a Raymond Gillis, but they've dropped the charges, so we have no directives to take you in."

"Raymond's dead?" she asked.

The officers were completely uninterested in her question. "Yeah, well, we actually stopped to tell you, Miss Conner, that we're looking for a homeless man, a Jimmy Newsome. He's about six feet tall, thin, in his late twenties, and has red hair.

Jimmy quietly stood up from the reading table across the main room and hid behind a bookshelf.

"He's apparently been stealing the communion wine from St Luke's and sneaking it into the Seniors' facility over off Reno avenue."

Simon spewed his coffee across the front desk, nodding his head with approving laughter. Gwen turned and managed to suppress hers, but then turned back. "Simon! Go get some paper towels and clean this mess up."

"Gwen, can I go back with him and sit down for a while?" Lisa asked. She was still trying to process the news that Raymond was dead.

Gwen sobered immediately.

"Of course you can, dear. I'll come back and check on you as soon as I'm done here."

"Well, we'd like your help finding him Miss Conner..."

"It's Mrs. Conner."

"Sorry, Mrs. Conner. Anyway, we'd like your help."

"I'm sorry, but that's not my job," she said.

They looked at one another and then back at her.

"I'm not turning this place into a trap to catch people for you. Those with nowhere to go see this library as a safe space, and I intend to keep it that way. You two seem to need telling this over and over. It's a public library, and I assume you have the right to come in and look around, but I'm not handing people over to you."

"That's fine *Mrs.* Conner," the one said. "We'll find him with or without your help." They both scanned the library. "We'll be back," said the other.

"You're welcome anytime," Gwen replied. "Maybe next time you might consider taking a book home with you. It's what we do here."

And they left.

Simon came back with the paper towels. "Sorry Gwen, but you gotta admit, that's priceless."

Gwen laughed. "I know, he's a sweet soul to do that, and he's right over there, hiding behind the reference section bookshelf."

"I'll let him know he's safe here."

"Thanks, Simon. I'm gonna go back and check on Lisa."

"We need to get this girl up the hill!"

"What's wrong Mary?"

"She's going into labor, Briena. Can you help me?"

Briena ran over to Mary's tent. "Come on Grace, we'll get you up to the shop. Jasmine will know what to do."

Everyone stopped what they were doing and gathered around Mary's tent. "Is she gonna be alright?" Monday asked.

"She'll be fine," Mary said, "we just need to get her up that hill."

Rookie put his bag down. "I'll run ahead of you and tell Jasmine so she can be ready."

"Thanks Rookie," Grace said, as she struggled to her feet with the help of Mary and Briena.

Rookie ran hard up the hill.

"Are you okay?" Gwen asked.

"Yeah, I'm okay, just trying to figure it all out. Honestly, Gwen, I know this sounds awful, but if he's really dead, I'm glad, and I truly had nothing to do with it. He was mixed up with some bad guys, and he probably got what he deserved."

"I believe you Lisa, and this sounds awful too, but with all that you've told me, I wouldn't have blamed you if you had."

"Yeah. Well, I guess I know why they were after me now. I'm glad it's over, and I'm glad I don't have to worry about him coming back into my life and making things hard for me and Jaime. That's been on my mind."

Gwen leaned back against the doorframe, folded her arms, and looked out the window blinds. "Nona's been hard at work."

Lisa nodded her head and pulled her hair back. "She needs to work on her timing though. Please, Nona, if you're actually out there and listening, thank you, but can I get off this rollercoaster now!"

Gwen laughed, "I'm sorry, it's not funny, but I do think it's over, dear. You leave tomorrow at one o'clock, and I'm gonna miss you, but I know he's there, waiting for you."

"Thank you so much, Gwen. I'm gonna miss you, too. But he's not waiting for me, he's waiting for a letter from me. I told him I'd write him, but when my plans changed, I thought I'd get back before a letter would. I can't imagine what he's thinking."

"Well, I can. He's probably thinking he'll get a letter soon. Lisa, it's only been what, three or four days since you left?"

"Yeah, it seems like forever though."

"I'm sure it does to him, too. Hey, I have an idea."

"What?"

"Let's have one last girl's night tonight and try really hard not to worry about the things we can't control. Your abuser's gone forever, your love is a day away, and I'm gonna order a large pizza for us."

Lisa turned her eyes towards Gwen and closed them with a soft laugh. She moved through the relief and then to Gwen's attempt at lightening the moment and nodded her head. "Sure, I'm always up for that. And I haven't had pizza in forever. Gwen?"

"Yes?"

"Can I just hang out here and then go home with you? I don't trust those guys."

"Who? The police?"

"Yeah."

"I don't blame you. And of course you can."

"Thank you."

"Oh, and look over on the magazine rack, there should be a television guide. Maybe you can find us a good movie to watch tonight."

Rookie burst through the front door of the shop. "Jasmine, is Jaime here?"

"No, he's gone into the mountains for the night, what's the matter Rookie?"

Just then, Cyril came in through the back, and Rookie dropped to the floor.

"Where's Jaime?" Cyril asked.

"He, uh, left a note that his, uh, his car wouldn't start. Yeah, his car wouldn't start, but that he'd be in as soon as it did."

"Really? So you're saying he managed to get to work to leave a note, but couldn't get to work? Help me understand that Jasmine."

Jasmine took too long to answer.

"Whenever he gets his car started and comes in, tell him he's fired."

Rookie winced.

"Cyril, give him a break. It's only one day, and I need his help."

"Can you explain the note?"

"I was covering for him. You wanna fire me too?"

Cyril crossed his arms.

"He's spending the day in the mountains, Cyril. Can you just let him have that?"

Rookie was on the floor, looking out the front window at Mary, Briena, Imani, and Grace who were coming up the road. Jasmine was glancing over at him from behind the counter. Cyril's view of him was blocked by the wall.

"Hurry!" Rookie motioned with his mouth to Jasmine.

"Look, I need to get this delivery back here stocked, Cyril. Just do what you're gonna do and let me get back to work."

They were crossing the road with Grace. Rookie made a pleading gesture with his hands. Cyril looked down at his pocket watch.

"Okay, he can stay. But make it clear to him that he checks with me before he takes off again! This is my shop, and..."

"Yes, yes, I know, Cyril," Jasmine said as she ushered him out the back door, just as Imani was opening the front.

"Rookie, why are you on the floor?" Mary asked. "And where's Jasmine?"

CHAPTER 24

I'll Need You to Come Downstairs

Lisa had dozed off. The loud knock, and a shout from the other side of the door, startled her awake.

"Pizza!"

She raised up and looked wide-eyed at Gwen. "Is it the police!"

Gwen reached over and turned the music down. "No dear, he said, 'pizza'. The pizza's here!"

Lisa slid back down into a relaxed position on the sofa and chased the panic of a last minute disaster out of her head.

Gwen gave the boy a generous tip, closed the door behind her, and the smell of pepperoni filled the room. She sat it on the coffee table and looked at Lisa. "Well?"

Lisa reached over and lifted the box top. "It looks delicious, Gwen. Thanks!"

"You're welcome, Lisa, and it's gonna be alright. You're only hours away, and I'm gonna keep you safe until you get on that bus."

"Thank you, Gwen. The last few days haven't been easy."

"I know."

They both sat still.

Gwen broke the silence. "I'll get plates and napkins."

Lisa jumped up from the sofa. "I'll help!" She turned the music back up as she followed. "Hey Gwen, do you have any more of that really sweet tea?"

"I do. The pitcher's in the fridge, and I'll have one too, if you're pouring."

"It's like syrup," Lisa said with a chuckle. "I love it." She filled the two glasses with ice and began singing along to Smokey Robinson, who was on the turntable.

Gwen looked over at her and smiled. "So! Did you find out what the eight o'clock movie is tonight?"

"Oh! Yeah, it's *Sleeping Beauty*. I've heard about it, but I've never seen it. What do you think?"

"I love that movie! Love conquers all."

"What?"

"You'll see."

Lisa nodded while she danced across the kitchen.

"Oh, and should I get the ketchup out for your pizza?"

Lisa collapsed onto the countertop in laughter, nearly spilling their drinks.

Gwen laughed with her. "Nah, sounds gross."

Lisa waited for it, lifted her head, and then sang with Smokey, "I second that emotion!"

Gwen threw her head back in laughter and walked into the living room. "So, if you feel like giving me a lifetime of devotion..."

Lisa fell into a lean against the refrigerator. "I second that emotion," she said to herself, as she remembered holding onto Jaime.

"Get up off the floor Rookie. What are you doing down there?" Imani asked as Jasmine closed the back door behind her.

"It's alright guys, he's gone."

Rookie climbed to his feet. "Cyril came in the back door. I had to hide!"

Mary and Briena struggled to help Grace through the narrow aisle. "Jasmine, this is our friend Grace, can she come back and sit down for a minute?" Mary asked.

"Of course she can. Are you okay?"

"I don't know. I think I'm going into labor."

"So, Jaime's not here?"

"No Imani, he's taken the day and night and gone into the mountains." Jasmine pulled a chair out for Grace. "I think we should get her to the hospital though, don't you?"

Mary leaned against the wall exhausted. "Yes. We were hoping maybe Jaime could take her."

"Well, I can, and I have room for y'all too if you want to come."

"We can't," Imani said, "the cops came down this morning and told us we had to clear out by this evening. We've gotta go back and pack everything up."

"What!"

Jasmine looked over at Mary who hung her head and nodded.

"What are you gonna do? Where are you gonna go? It's supposed to get so cold tonight."

Rookie pulled a soft drink from the cooler and held it up, Jasmine nodded, he opened it and took a drink. "A few of us are gonna bed down in the parking garage for the night."

Imani reached into her pockets. "Mary and I are gonna try the mission."

"Why don't y'all go to the mission too, Rookie? Seems like it'd be warmer than the garage."

"I'm banned."

"Banned?" Jasmine asked, with a pained expression.

"Yeah, lots of folks are," Mary said.

Imani was counting her change. "And then there are a lot of folks who would rather face the cold than to spend a night in there."

"Or even a night in jail!" Rookie said as he downed the last of his soda, "at least the jailers are nice to you."

Grace doubled over and moaned, "I'm scared, guys."

"Hey, we'd better get her taken care of. If I help, do you think you can make it to my car Grace? It's just out back and down a few steps."

"Yeah, I think so."

"Okay, here, take my arm." Jasmine turned. "I wish there were something I could do for ya'll. This is awful. I feel so helpless."

"We'll be okay," Rookie said, "but thanks, Jasmine."

"Pick out some groceries for the night while I get Grace into the car. I'll have to come back in and lock up the shop behind you."

"Thank you, Jasmine."

"Oh…" She grabbed a pack of cigarettes from the back rack and tossed them to Rookie. "Take these with you, too!"

They filled a few grocery bags and began their walk back to camp.

Mary and Imani stood in the line that stretched from the mission's check-in counter to the street outside. It had been months since either of them had stayed there, but they agreed to try and manage it for one night. Forty-five minutes after arriving, they finally reached the counter where they were asked to hand over their bags. Their tents and blankets had been stashed by the back porch of the shop, where Cyril had found them about thirty minutes later and burned them in the fire pit.

"When do we get these back?" Mary asked.

The woman at the counter cut a condescending eye at her. "When we give them to you."

"In the morning, before breakfast," said the young man collecting them.

"Move along," the woman snapped, "you're not the only one's trying to get in here. It's been a long day, and some of us would like to go home."

Imani and Mary looked at one another. "We would too," Mary said, as they turned towards the chapel.

"You just watch your mouth, or you can go right back outside!" the woman shouted.

They shook their heads, found two folding chairs together, and waited to be called into the cafeteria for supper.

"I'm worried, Imani," Mary whispered.

"Why?"

"Last time I was here, we just put our bags on our assigned bunks. I'm sure they're gonna go through them, and I've got a bottle in one of mine." Mary was ringing her hands. "I don't want to go to jail."

"Maybe they won't."

"They will."

"Well, even if they do, it's not like you're drunk. I mean, they'd probably just throw it away and give you a warning. Don't you think?"

"I don't know, Imani. I just wanna get this night over with and get into my new home tomorrow."

Mary was trying to chase the panic of a last minute disaster out of her head, but it wasn't easy.

"I know you do, Mary." Imani took her hand, "let's say a prayer together," they bowed their heads. "Dear..."

"Jesus Christ! It's getting cold out here."

Jaime stood up from his knees, cupped his hands over his breath, and looked up at the stars. He was finally giving up on a fire. The woods were just too wet, and he hadn't come prepared for these freezing temperatures. He only had the clothes he was wearing. His boots and pants were wet from the stream crossing, and there was no way of drying them now. He looked over at his tent and debated whether to crawl into his sleeping bag or pack up and get out while he still could. He'd have to hike out in the dark, but the sky was clear, and the moon was bright. "The stream," he thought, "I'd have to wade the stream in the dark." He slowly dropped back down to his knees, unzipped the door to his tent, and sat down. He pulled his boots and pants off, and set them in the corner, and slid into his cold sleeping bag.

Prince Phillip looked over the cliff at the Sword of Truth below. Maleficent was gone, and with this last battle won, he could now go to Princess Aurora. And that was the last she remembered.

"Lisa," Gwen gently pulled the bowl of popcorn from her hands. "Wake up dear, let's get you in bed. You have a long day ahead of you tomorrow."

"Wait!" Lisa was so sleepy, she felt drugged. "What happened?"

"You fell asleep."

"No! I mean, I missed the end of the movie. What happened? Did he get back to Aurora in time?"

"Goodnight, Mary," Imani said with a hug. "They've put me way down on the other end of the hall. I'll see you in the morning, though."

"Goodnight, Imani. Sleep well dear."

Mary was preparing her blankets when he walked up. "Excuse me, is this yours?"

She turned and saw him holding out her bag. "Yes sir, it is." Her heart was in her throat.

"I'll need you to come downstairs with me."

"Can I tell my friend that I'm..."

He took her by the arm. "No, come now, please."

The night warden escorted Mary out the front door. "I hope you'll pray to the Lord Jesus and ask forgiveness."

Mary solemnly wrapped her coat around herself, and thought about what to do, as her breath crystalized before her. "I pray the Lord's forgiveness every night. Tonight won't be any different," she said to the warden, as he closed the door behind her.

She walked down the sidewalk towards the shop where she'd left her blankets. She would have enough to make it through the night, and she could crawl underneath the back porch until morning when Jasmine would come in for work.

The nurse took Grace back to the delivery room. "This baby's coming soon, dear. Is this your first?"

"Yes, ma'am."

"Well, there's no need to be scared. It'll be alright. Nona will be in soon. You're baby's in good hands. Would you like to stay with your friend?" she asked Jasmine.

"Nona? Who is that?" Grace asked.

"Deep breaths dear. I said, Dr. McNeil. He's the best."

Grace paused and reluctantly accepted that she'd heard the nurse wrong. The contractions started again. "Please, Jasmine? Can you stay with me?" Grace screamed through her clenched jaws.

"Breathe Grace!" the nurse said as she took her pulse.

"I'll stay, Grace. I've never done this before either, but I'll stay." Jasmine took Grace's other hand.

"Where's the father?" the nurse asked, as she made notes on her clipboard.

"I hope he's in hell!" Grace shouted.

The nurse chuckled and Jasmine smiled, but then winced in pain, as Grace squeezed her hand.

Mary hurried to the back of the shop. She was startled to see that her blankets and tent were gone. "Cyril." She desperately hunted around the building, and all through the parking lot, and then turned with a glare at the charred remains on the fire pit. "How can people be so evil?" She wasn't asking with any malice, her heart was pure, she was asking with a genuine desire to understand.

Almost with a childlike naiveté, she couldn't understand hatefulness, because she'd never really felt it before. Mary knew anger, a righteous anger, but she'd never really felt hatred. She looked up at the back door. "I'm sure it's locked," but she climbed the steps anyway. And it was. She sat down and cupped her hands over her breath and then warmed them under her arms. She took the bottle of vodka from her bag and turned it up with a violent shiver. She knew what she had to do. It was a long walk, and she was already so tired, but she had to try and make it to the garage. Carol and Rookie had loaded all of their belongings into shopping carts and would have plenty of bedding and blankets to share with her.

Lisa offered to take the pizza box out. She opened the door, and her eyes were arrested by the full moon. She stood on the steps and wondered where Jaime was.

Jaime was restless. He couldn't stop wondering why Lisa hadn't written, and if she loved him like he loved her. He unzipped his tent door and looked up at the full moon.

Mary stopped to rest under the bridge before trying to make the long walk to the garage. She lethargically looked up at the full moon and then closed her eyes.

CHAPTER 25

No Time For Long Goodbyes

Jaime pulled on the handbrake, looked over at the shop, and then at his watch. It would be another hour before Jasmine arrived for work, so he decided to walk down to the campsite and tell Mary about his night in the mountains. It was cold and overcast. He looked around at the familiar skies that brought the Appalachian rains, zipped his jacket up to his neck, and sprinted across the street. As he walked towards the church on the hill, he couldn't resist the feeling that things seemed different than they did before he'd left. It wasn't the light on some Damascus road, but it was as though a veil had been lifted. He felt a lightening of his soul. He was tired, and his pants and boots were still wet from crossing the stream, but he walked along the church grounds with a sense of urgency. He reached the crest of the hill, looked down at the campsite, and froze in place.

"I'm freezing in this place, Rookie."

"I know, me too."

"Let's go to the shop and warm up, maybe Jasmine will be there, and we can get some coffee."

"Okay."

"Bombay!" Carol called out.

"Yes, Carol?"

"Wanna go to the shop and get some coffee with us?"

"Yes, please. What will we do with our possibles?"

"Our what?"

"Our possibles, our…"

"You mean, our stuff?" Rookie asked.

Bombay looked over his shoulder and then turned back over. "Yes, our *stuff*," he said under his breath.

"We'll just leave everything here in the corner. It's what we always do. Nobody ever bothers them. Besides, Rookie and I are coming back tonight."

Bombay looked back over at them. "Jasmine said it's supposed to start raining today and…"

"Yeah, and it's gonna rain through 'til Friday!" Rookie said as he started rolling up his sleeping bag.

"What about you Shelly? Wanna go with us?"

"I'm gonna go up to the corner for a while," she said from underneath her blankets, "when it warms up a bit."

"Be careful, Shelly," Bombay said, as he reluctantly lifted his stiff body from the concrete floor. "These soldiers are hard on us beggars."

"They're policemen," Carol said with a laugh.

Bombay held up his bottle of mouthwash to see how much was left. "They seem like soldiers to me."

"I don't care," Shelly mumbled, "at least I'll be warm and dry in jail."

Everything was gone. Jaime cupped his hands over his breath and tried making sense of what he was seeing. He walked down the hill and into the campsite, sat down on the log by the fire ring, lit a cigarette, and wondered, "Where'd they all go?" They're being run out by the city had never crossed his mind. "Mary gets her house today," he thought. "But even if they were all helping her move in, they wouldn't have packed up their stuff." He wandered throughout the site looking for anything, but there was no trace. "Something's not right here." He crushed his cigarette out on the tree beside him and made his way up the hill and back to the shop.

Imani took her tray and made her way through the crowded cafeteria, looking for Mary.

"Joker, have you seen Mary? She came in with me last night and…"

"They put her out, Imani. I saw it. Nine o'clock, just before lights out. I was on laundry detail, and I saw them escorting her out the front door."

Imani froze. "It was so cold last night! How could they do that!"

"Oh, I saw 'em put five or six out. They put Paddy out, too."

"Paddy in the wheelchair!"

"Yep."

Imani threw her tray across the room and screamed.

"Ma'am!" The woman called out from behind the serving station.

"Shut up! Y'all not gonna throw *me* out! I'm leaving, and I will NEVER step foot in this place again!"

Imani stormed out of the cafeteria.

Joker began striking the table with his plastic cup, and within seconds, the whole cafeteria had joined him.

The morning warden ran up the stairs. "Stop it! Stop it now, or you can all go out! Don't make me call the police!"

"Do the people who give money to this place know ya'll throw us out into the cold in the name of Jesus!" Joker called out.

"Yeah! Where's Paddy?" Amy shouted.

The cafeteria erupted in chants of, "Where's Paddy?"

Imani marched past the check in clerk where one of the staff members reached out to take her by the arm.

"Get your fuckin' hands off me!" she shouted into his face, jerking her arm out of his grasp. She stopped, looked him dead in his eyes, and shoved his chest with both hands, throwing him back into the counter. She slammed open the front door, dropped her bag on the sidewalk, and dug through it. She pulled her scarf out and scanned the street as she wrapped up. "The shop," she thought to herself, "that's where Mary would've gone last night." She threw her bag over her shoulder and started the walk.

Gwen pulled into a parking space, turned the ignition off, sat back, and turned towards Lisa.

"This is it."

Lisa couldn't stop smiling.

"I want you to have this." Gwen reached over and put a folded wad of bills in Lisa's hand.

"But…"

"I'm not taking 'no' for an answer." She folded Lisa's fingers around it, and warmly clasped Lisa's hand within the both of hers. "And here's a letter of recommendation too."

"I don't know what to say, Gwen."

"It's okay, you don't need to say anything. You're gonna need some spending money. You've got a long ride ahead of you."

"No. I mean, yes, thank you for the money and the letter, but I don't know what to say. You've done so much for me, and I guess I don't really understand why."

Gwen took the keys from the ignition and began fidgeting with them in her lap. "Lisa, you're the first person I've loved since my Bobby left. I guess I don't really understand why either. But I've given up trying. I think maybe love is a problem we'll never solve. We just embrace it, enjoy the moments, and hope it never goes away."

Lisa took Gwen's hand.

"I love you too, Gwen, and I'm sorry for going away…"

"No, no, no, Lisa. My love for you is going nowhere. You may be leaving, but not my love for you."

Lisa wiped away a tear.

"Because I love you, I want nothing more than for you to go. Our love for each other is a deep caring friendship. What you feel for Jaime is something beyond that, and I want that for you more than anything."

Gwen reached into her coat pocket and handed her a tissue. Lisa blew her nose and nodded.

"Besides, I'm sure we'll be writing each other every day!"

Lisa let out a laugh through her tears. "Yeah, I'm really good at that, aren't I?"

They both laughed and leaned in together, burying their faces into each other's necks.

"Okay, no time for long goodbyes," Gwen said with a smile. "If you miss this bus…"

"I'm not gonna!" Lisa reached over and quickly kissed Gwen on the cheek and swung her door open. "Let's go!"

"Here's Jasmine!" Carol said through her cupped hands.

Jasmine pulled in to see Carol, Rookie, Imani, Jaime, and Bombay standing in a circle at the foot of the steps. She got out of the car and pulled her coat in tight.

"Sorry guys," Jasmine said. "Grace had her baby girl last night around ten o'clock, and I stayed with her for a bit. It's been a long night."

"So it's a girl?" Rookie asked.

"Yeah, her name's Mary, 'cause she's full of Grace."

Carol smiled, closed her eyes, and crossed herself.

Jaime shuffled his feet. "How long you been working on that line, Jasmine?" he asked with a devilish grin.

"Shut up, Jaime. I'm just barely in the mood for you."

"Yeah, well…"

"I said shut up, Jaime."

Everyone laughed through their stiffened shivers.

Jasmine closed the car door. "Hey! Let's get inside and make some coffee! Where's Mary?"

"We don't know," Rookie said as he put his cigarette out.

They all followed Jasmine into the shop.

Carol was the last to come in. "Oh, it feels so good in here."

"I'll get the coffee on. So Imani, didn't you and Mary stay at the mission last night?"

Imani slid down with her back against the wall and into a sitting position on the floor.

"She was thrown out."

Jaime turned with furrowed brows. "What!"

Imani rubbed the heels of her hands into her eyes. "They found a bottle in her bag, I guess, and put her out. I don't know where she went or where she is. That's why I came here. I figured she'd come after her blankets."

"But they're all gone," Rookie said.

"They're gone?" Jasmine asked.

Jaime lit a cigarette. "Wait, what blankets, what are y'all talking about? And why were you in the mission? And what happened to the campsite?"

Carol reached for a coffee cup. "The cops came yesterday morning, Jaime, and told us we had to clear out."

"Mary and I decided to stay at the mission."

"And some of us went to the garage by the bus station."

Jasmine started pouring everyone's coffee. "I told Imani and Mary they could store their blankets and tents under the back porch. So Imani, are you saying they're gone? I came in so fast I hadn't noticed."

"Yeah Jasmine, they're gone."

Jaime tapped his ashes into the sink. "So surely Mary would've come to get her blankets, but they're not there. So what does she do?"

Everyone stood still.

"Did she know y'all were in the garage, Carol?"

"Yeah."

"So she would've probably started to make her way..."

Jaime set his cup down, ran out the back door, and stopped on the porch. He scanned the immediate area around the shop, and then out and beyond until he saw what looked like someone sleeping at the foot of the overpass abutment. He recognized Mary's coat. He closed his eyes as the muscles in his face relaxed and his shoulders dropped. The universe was dissolving.

"Please, no. How could you do this to her."

He staggered down the steps, holding onto the railing, crying, and trembling with fear.

"Really, Nona?" Lisa asked as she boarded the bus. The nameplate on the driver read, 'Samson.' "You're just being cute now." She walked down the aisle and found a window seat in the back. Gwen was standing on the sidewalk blowing her a kiss. Lisa blushed and blew one back. She slid her window down. "I'll write!"

Gwen set her hands on her hips, and they both laughed.

"I really will!" she said.

"I know, I know. I'm just teasing you!"

The door closed and the bus bucked as it found its first gear and started pulling away. Gwen ran along beside it.

"Only twelve hours!" she shouted.

"I know!" Lisa called back.

Gwen slowed. She was out of breath but managed to reach out with her hand.

Lisa placed her hand on the window to match Gwen's, and then breathed a sigh of relief as she collapsed into the seat. She closed her eyes and thought back to the kitchen that...

Jaime was raging through and throwing the chairs into the walls. Just like Ezra, he had been baited into the trap of thinking that maybe there was some meaning to life. Maybe some design or purpose, maybe some wizard behind the curtain, but only to have his neck broken as he reached for it.

"I've been a god damned fool!" He fell into his bed, buried his face in his pillow, and sobbed, "I've been a god damned fool!" Mary was gone. And only hours before her dream was to come true. He felt a tap on his shoulder and looked over to see his box cutter being handed to him. This time, however, Ezra wasn't laughing or mocking, he had a look of empathy for Jaime.

"This razor will make things right. It's the only truth."

Jaime took it and turned his face back into his pillow.

"I'll do it, just give me some time."

"Use it. Don't step in front of a train. You don't wanna know what that last second of indecision feels like." Ezra crawled up the wall and back into the ceiling through the missing tile.

"Hypothermia," The paramedic said.

"What's that?" Rookie asked.

"She died from being too cold. Looks like sometime around ten o'clock. Do any of you know why she was sleeping under this bridge on such a cold night?"

Imani crossed her legs, and threw a stone across the way, as her angry crying had exhausted itself. "She was put out of the mission last night!"

"What!"

Carol cupped her hands over her breath and looked over at the two police officers. "Yeah, y'all busted up our camp yesterday, and we had to find shelter last night. Mary went with Imani to the mission and they threw her out 'cause she had a bottle in her bag!"

The two officers looked at one another and shook their heads. "We're sorry y'all. We had nothing to do with that, and didn't even know it was going down," one officer said.

"Yeah, we know y'all got it rough out here," said the other, "and we're sorry about your friend. She didn't deserve this. Where will you all stay tonight? It's not gonna be as cold, but the rain's coming."

Carol was kicking her feet against the ground, trying to warm her toes. "A few of us will be in the garage by the bus station."

The officers looked at each other and then at the group. "That's on our beat. We'll come by and check on y'all tonight."

"And bring you hot coffee," said the other.

Jasmine stared through Mary, who was lying under a sheet, cold and still on the ground. "You said you think she died around ten o'clock last night?"

The paramedics were packing up their bags. "Yeah, I mean, we can't be precise, but that's what it looks like," the other nodded in agreement.

Bombay looked at Jasmine. "But you said it was around that time that Mary was born."

Jasmine never broke her stare. "It was."

CHAPTER 26

I See You're a Doctor of Some Sort

Jasmine let it ring and ring before finally hanging up. She'd finished dinner, pushed her plate aside, and picked up the phone to check on Jaime, but he wasn't answering. He'd walked away from the site where they had found Mary that morning, without a word, and looking even more dead inside than usual. She put the dishes away, grabbed her car keys, and left to go try and find him.

Jaime wandered through the crowds in the square, mesmerized by the absurdity of it all. He leaned his back against a wall and slid down into a sitting position, with his knees in his chest and his arms wrapped around them.

"God loves you!" said the man handing out leaflets.

"God's dead," replied the young woman, who took one and crumpled it up in his face.

"He was never alive," Jaime mumbled, as she walked past him.

She reached down and slipped him a few dollars. "Right on, man."

"No! I don't need this, I wasn't..."

"Keep it, you're cool."

"But I don't need... Wait!"

"Keep it!" she said looking back.

"But I'm not..." He looked around appealing to those walking past him, "But I'm not..."

He opened his hand, and the cash fell to the ground. He stood up and drifted into a nearby alley.

"Where you goin'?"

"Tennessee."

"Me too. Family there?"

Lisa hesitated to say.

"Oh, I'm sorry. I didn't mean to pry. My name's Ezra by the way, business trip. Well, I'm going there to make sure someone finishes something they..."

"Lisa. My name's Lisa."

"I know."

She was instantly uncomfortable with him. "Excuse me, ma'am."

"Yes?" The attendant replied as she was making her way down the aisle checking tickets.

"Could I get a blanket?"

"Of course you can. Give me just a few minutes, dear."

Lisa bent over and placed her book into her bag that was on the floor between her feet. "I'm gonna try and get some sleep," she said, without looking over at him.

Nona handed the ticket back to the passenger seated some three rows forward, looked back at Ezra dead in the eyes, and motioned with her head for him to leave. He stood up and squeezed past her through the aisle.

"Better weave fast, love. I'll get to that garage before she does."

Lisa zipped her bag and raised her head. Ezra was gone.

"There you are!"

Jaime was sitting against a dumpster in an alley off the square, with two others, when Jasmine walked up. "Can I steal this guy away from y'all for a minute?" They both looked up at her and nodded their heads. Jaime looked away, but she wasn't having it.

"Jaime!"

He looked up at her as she walked over. "Excuse me," and she sat down beside him.

"I'm not letting you do this."

"Do what?" he asked, as he reached into his pocket for a cigarette.

Jasmine moved over and pressed her shoulder into his. "Stop it. You know what."

Jaime dragged deep from his cigarette and stared into the asphalt bed between his legs.

"I'm not doing anything Jasmine but talking over plans with my new best friends here."

"Plans?"

"Yeah," one of them replied, "we're gonna buy a boat and..."

"Jaime!" Jasmine jumped up and grabbed him under his arm, pulling him to his feet. "Come over here with me!" She led him around the corner and pressed him into the wall. "A boat!"

Jaime tried looking away, but she chased his eyes down.

"I know your heart's breaking but stop hallucinating with these two! You're not gonna buy a fuckin' boat! Really? A boat! What the hell does that even mean? If I weren't so concerned about you right now, I'd be laughing my ass off, but I know you've been drinking, and you've let reality slip away from you. Come here."

She pulled him in and wrapped her arms around him.

"I'm not really gonna buy a boat."

"I know you're not, silly. But your new best friends think you are."

She felt his head nodding into her neck.

"It's getting late. What are you gonna do tonight? I'm worried about you."

Jaime looked over her shoulder at Ezra, who was standing at the rear of the ally. "I think I'm gonna go be with my mom."

"Now that sounds like a good idea. Is she close by?"

"She always is, I mean, yeah."

Streams of cold and worn souls were merging under the bridge to the sounds of the cheerful strains of *Oh Happy Day*, sung by an oblivious choir of enthusiastic fools.

Christians always seem to be drunk on the hopes of some disembodied heaven, to the detriment of this hell on earth. Heaven on earth could be done, but that would mean reaching back into their holy book and recapturing the beauty of the first Jesus community, who sold everything they had, and shared all things collected in common so that no one would do without. But times had changed, and Christianity had become the bride of the Western economic and political systems. Those without would continue to do without, because they were allegedly too lazy to do better, and those privileged with, would ration out to them *almost* enough to survive on until *We All Get to Heaven*.

It was Wednesday night, mid-week forgiveness for those who were too sinful to wait for the following Sunday, and a mid-week feel good boost to those with plenty and who didn't need it. But the poor were hungry. And that's really why they came. The food was a lure, I mean, who's gonna actually come out of the comfort of their tent, and walk to a service, only to be told that you're a sinner 'cause you drink to cope with your hopelessness? Christianity is a toxic fraud, but Jesus was legit. It's not enough for comfortable suburbanites to love a comfortable Jesus. This world needs systems that look like the fed up Jesus. And until then, the poor would be grateful for their rations.

They walked with their trays to the folding tables and chairs.

"I wonder how Jaime's doing," Carol asked, "he seemed really upset this morning. I don't think he's used to this."

"Us dying?" Monday asked. Briena squeezed his hand tight. "Yeah."

Bombay searched his plate for something worthy of eating. "I saw him earlier in town, he didn't look well. He gave me a bottle, and without a word, he walked on."

Jasmine walked up to the table. "Hey guys, I just wanted to come out and check on everybody. I know the last couple of days have been really hard. Looks like you're all here though. Y'all got places to stay tonight? It won't be as cold, but the rain's coming soon."

"Yeah, we'll be in the garage again tonight. After the rain passes, we'll set up a new campsite somewhere," Monday said.

Jasmine took a deep breath and slowly exhaled. Humans living in garages and in the woods had not yet been normalized with her, and never would be.

"You heard from Jaime?" Carol asked, "we're kinda worried about him."

Jasmine refocused. "Yeah, I checked in with him earlier. Sounds like he's gonna be okay. He's going to stay with his mother tonight."

Briena looked up. "He said he was gonna go stay with his mom?"

"Yeah, well, he said he was going to be with his ..."

Imani froze. "Jasmine, Jaime's mom is dead."

"What?"

"She died when he was young."

Briena put down her drink. "Did he say he was going to *stay* with his mom or *be* with his mom?"

Jasmine thought back. "Oh my god!" She pushed the youth group server out of the way and ran to her car.

The sound of thunder signaled it was time for the rest of them to leave too. They needed to get to the garage before the rain started falling.

"Excuse me."

"Yes?"

"I see you're a doctor of some sort?" Nona asked.

"Well, I'm a paramedic, not a doctor. We help in emergency situations. Is everything okay?"

"Not exactly. Just a while ago, I passed a young man in the garage off Seventeenth Avenue, over by the bus station, and he didn't seem well at all. I'm sorry, I didn't mean to interrupt your coffee break. I just thought..."

"Oh no, you're right to say something. That's where some of our homeless friends sleep."

"It looked like he might have been cutting himself."

"William!"

"Yeah?"

"Wanna run over to Seventeenth and check on someone?"

"Sure! Let's do it."

"Thank you both so much! It may be nothing, but I'd hate for him to be gone before Lisa gets there."

"Sorry? Lisa?"

"Oh dear, I have someone on my mind. I meant before *you* get there."

"We'll head that way now and check on him. And by the way, that's a beautiful comforter you're weaving."

The bus came to a stop, waking Lisa from a deep sleep.

"We're here folks. It's one thirty-five a.m. local time. It's a bit cold and rainy, as you can see, so be careful exiting the bus. Thank you for traveling with us and be sure to collect all your bags and belongings."

Lisa stretched, reached down for her bag on the floor, and looked out the window to see someone running frantically out from the garage across the street calling for help.

"Wait!" she thought. "That's the man that..."

Bombay scanned the area just outside the garage entrance, tearing his shirt open and panting when he saw Lisa looking at him from the bus window.

"Come now!" He motioned wildly with his hands. "Hurry! Your Jaime, he is dying!"

"What!?" Lisa fought her way through the aisle. "I'm sorry, I have to get off!" She leapt from the top step and ran across the street to the sound of horns blowing.

"We need a doctor!" Bombay cried out. "He's bleeding! This way." Bombay took her by the hand and ran towards the back corner of the garage, and there he was, propped up against the wall, arms extended out and blood everywhere.

Lisa gasped, "No!" She dropped to her knees and lunged into his chest, wrapping her arms around his neck. "No, Jaime!" She buried her face into his neck and began sobbing, "Please don't go."

The paramedics pulled into the garage and rushed over to the corner where everyone was huddled.

"He's over here," Lisa cried out, "please save him."

"Let go of him, dear. What's his name?"

"Jaime."

They both took an arm and began wrapping his wrists with bandages.

"Jaime! Can you hear me?

"He's in shock, William!"

Ezra was leaning against a dumpster and watching when he turned to see Nona coming down the alley that separated the bus station from the garage.

CHAPTER 27

Mon Trésor

"The what?"

Lisa looked over at Carol. "The ketchup, can you get the ketchup out?"

"Ketchup?"

Jaime was awakened by the sound of familiar voices. He climbed out of bed and followed them into the kitchen.

Lisa melted. "There he is." She gently hurried past everyone and wrapped her arms around his waist from behind. "And yeah, it's a thing," she said, resting her chin on his shoulder with a smile.

It was Saturday morning, and everyone had gathered into Jaime and Lisa's place for breakfast.

Monday looked up from his newspaper. "What's a thing?"

Jaime yawned and squinted his eyes. "What are y'all talking about?"

Imani took the percolator from the stovetop and started pouring everyone's coffee. "Lisa said to get the ketchup out."

"Yeah," Jaime said, as though it should've been obvious, "it's for the scrambled eggs."

The kitchen turned solemn. Everyone's eyes collectively unfocused, but then discreetly searched one another out, making sure they weren't alone in hearing this madness. It was the same as when he would be talking to the invisible person at the campfire. Lisa saw it all, squeezed Jaime's waist, and chuckled as she buried her face into his neck. She felt the bandages wrapped around his wrists and shivered at the image of him lying broken and bleeding on that garage floor.

But he was here, and so was Carol. And she was never the shy one. "I thought I'd seen everything. I mean, I once saw a guy stir mustard up in his grits!"

Lisa nodded her head into Jaime's neck and was full on laughing. She pulled away and looked up at him.

"Please can I?" She was weakening with laughter.

Carol looked over at Lisa. "Don't tell me..."

"He does, Carol."

Jaime closed his eyes and shook his head, but they were spared the forthcoming lecture on, "What's a thing" by a knock at the door.

Rookie set his cup down. "I'll get it. It's probably Jasmine."

"Couldn't be," Lisa said, drying her eyes, "she went back to Memphis for the weekend."

"Oh, yeah." Rookie opened the door to the shouts of "Grace!" from everyone.

"Hey, y'all!"

"Aww! Who's this?" Monday asked.

"This is what makes my life worth living."

Jaime closed his eyes, nodded his head, and pulled Lisa's arms tighter around his waist.

"I looked for y'all at the garage. I wanted you to meet her, but Shelly said everybody was over here. I can only stay for just a minute though. My folks are waiting outside."

"What?" Rookie asked.

"Yeah, they're letting me come back home!"

"That's amazing Grace!"

Lisa reached around and covered Jaime's mouth.

"Isn't it funny how a grandbaby can cover a multitude of sins," she said laughing. "Is Jasmine here? I wanted to thank her. She probably saved my baby's life."

"She's not," Carol said. "But we can tell her when she gets back. She's just gone for the weekend."

"Please do, y'all."

Lisa whispered into Jaime's ear, "You wanna hold her?" She looked away before he answered, "What's her name, Grace?"

"It's Mary. And where *is* Mary? I thought she'd be here too. Oh, wait! I bet she's in her new place, isn't she?"

Lisa covered Jaime's mouth again before he could answer. She whispered into his ear, "Go hold her Jaime. It's Mary."

He closed his eyes as she gently nudged him forward.

"Can I ask why you didn't come forward with this information earlier? It's been nearly a week and a half."

"I don't git inna town that much, really. I keep ta myself up on that mountain, but it jest kept vexin me."

Chief Dodson leaned forward with her hands massaging her temples. "Okay, let me get this straight. You saw a Volkswagen Beetle, and what you thought was a thin young man throwing a body off into the river. The car I can understand, I guess, but it was dark. How are you able to describe this person? I know the place, and it's dark as hell."

"His lights were on. I done seen him."

"What direction were you looking from?"

"Huh?"

"What direction? From behind the car, or from in front?"

"From behind'im. What's tha difference."

"Because, if from the front, his headlights would not actually be shining on him. You would've seen nothing but his silhouette."

"His what?"

"Never mind. And what were *you* doing down there? If I may ask."

"I come down on some nights and sit aginst a tree above the river. I drink some, I confess, it ain't illegal yet though, and my wife don't know. So I hide the bottle by the tree and tell her I'm goin' for a short walk. Listen, I ain't proud of it, but this ain't what I've come inna town to talk to you'uns about. The Lord was givin' me visions, so I had to declare it."

Chief Dodson clasped her hands around the back of her neck, drawing her elbows forward. "Okay, well, you were right to do so. Let me ask you."

"Yes'em?"

"Do you think you would recognize this young man if you saw him? I mean, do you think you could pick him out from a lineup?"

"Yes'em, I think I could."

Jasmine had scraped together enough money to rent the space beside Jaime's for the first month. Lisa left the hospital Thursday afternoon and spent that evening, 'til the next morning, collecting her things, and setting fire to Raymond's. She moved into Jaime's place, cleaned, and decorated it with the flowers she'd picked from the empty lot at the end of the road. On Friday, Jasmine drove down to the garage, and in two trips, delivered the others to their new home. She picked up Imani and Bombay first, and then returned for Carol, Rookie, Briena, and Monday. No more garages and campsites. She had no idea where the money was going to come from for the following months, but she would figure that out later.

"You make really good chili, Carol!" Lisa said as she started collecting bowls.

"Why thank you, Lisa. My momma taught me. It's not too spicy, is it?"

"No! Not at all. It's perfect."

Monday jumped up off the floor. "I'll get those."

Imani laughed. "Monday's our expert dishwasher. Some reason, that boy loves to wash dishes. He had his own little station down by the stream. Sometimes he'd be down there for hours."

Briena looked away, her eyes were welling with tears.

"I used to be one over at Al's café. That's where me and Briena met. I don't know why I like it so much. Maybe it's the feeling of cleaning up a mess, or making things new, or putting something back the way it used to be." Monday was acting. He looked over at Briena for approval and saw her crying. That wasn't where they had met.

Ezra walked in and sat down. "It's about erasing your life. You messed up and you know it. Go ahead, you've been thinking about it ever since. Do it."

Lisa looked over at Monday with empathetic eyes.

Monday paused. "Who are you?"

Everyone looked at Monday. He nervously laughed. "I mean, are you done?" he said, as he reached for Rookie's bowl, and made his second trip to the sink. "I probably think too much. I know I talk too much!" He nervously looked back over his shoulder, but Ezra was gone.

"No, you don't Monday," Imani said, "I think that's beautiful. And I think you gotta good heart. We all make mistakes. Ignore the self-righteous, and all those things will be put right for you soon. I believe in you."

"Thanks, Imani." Monday looked over again to be sure.

"Now don't you go tearing up on us," she said with a sympathetic laugh. "We all know how sentimental you can get. You too Briena. Wait, why are you crying child?"

Briena took a deep breath. "I'm not, it's allergies."

Imani rolled her eyes and shook her head.

"Okay, I won't," Monday said, but he already had, and was drying the tears running down his cheeks with his shoulders, while carrying a stack of bowls.

Imani looked at one, then the other. "You two…"

"Here, let me help."

"Jaime!" everyone shouted.

Bombay grabbed the back of his shirt. "You can't get your wrappings wet, my friend."

"But I can dry, can't I?"

Lisa took him by the arm. "Come away from the dishwashing station, mon trésor, that's only going to lead to you hurting yourself. You got a thing for dishwashers?" she asked with a laugh.

"But..."

"What did you call him?" Carol asked.

"Mon trésor. It's French for my treasure."

Jaime walked back over to the sink.

"Why do they call you 'Monday'?" Jaime asked.

Monday looked down into the sink and released a bitter laugh. "Cause everyone hates Mondays."

Jaime looked at him, searched his face, and wondered.

"Not everyone," Briena said under her breath.

Lisa rested her hand on Jaime's shoulder. "You look like you're getting tired love, just relax, sit here and let me pour you a vodka. You need to get into bed soon."

"But I gotta..."

"No, the only thing you gotta do is get your sleep. Please, darling, let me help you get better."

Jaime brushed Lisa's hair from her face and looked into her eyes. She was home and flooding his heart. Maybe for the first time ever, but at least for as long as he could remember, life felt worth living. Christian ideas of heaven – eternally praising some white-bearded man with a harp, could not compare with this.

"Actually," she said, "let's just go on back now." Lisa took his hand and led him towards the bedroom. She turned the lights down and pulled back the covers. "I'll put a record on. What are you in the mood for?"

He had that faraway look in his eyes.

"I know, Percy Faith." Lisa set the needle down and slow-danced over to the sound of *Moon River*. She covered him with blankets and kissed him.

"Lisa."

"I'll be right back, Jaime. I need to see to our friends."

"I know."

She started back towards the kitchen.

"Lisa."

"Yes?"

"I love you so much."

She ran back to the bed and wrapped herself into him. "Jaime..."

"Hey, you two!" Carol was standing in the doorway.

Jaime raised up, and Lisa looked over. "I'm coming, Carol."

She kissed him again and rolled off the bed. "I *will* be back, just let me see our friends out."

"He's tired y'all," Lisa said, as she walked back into the kitchen. "Help yourselves. There's no shortage of vodka in this house," she said, with a full eye roll and a laugh. "We're just measuring his until he heals. And he needs to sleep, so y'all are welcome to stay as long as you like, but I'm going back to be with him."

Bombay took the measuring cup from the cabinet and looked over at Lisa. "Où avez-vous appris le français?"

Lisa spun around stunned. "Bombay! This woman I used to cook and clean for taught me, back in Santa Fe. And you?"

With shaking hands, Bombay carefully measured Jaime's cup of vodka, and said, without breaking his focus, "I studied it at university, in Delhi."

"I'm sorry Bombay."

"For what?"

"For everything."

"I accept that you're sorry Lisa, but you have no part in this."

Lisa walked over to Bombay. "I understand, but can I ask? Who does?"

"One day soon."

Lisa nodded.

He handed Lisa the measured cup. "Go care for him and I'll move everyone quietly out."

The dishes were done, and Bombay was quietly ushering everyone through the bedroom and to the front door.

"You need to replace that ceiling tile, Jaime. God only knows what might crawl outta there one night," Carol said.

Jaime never opened his eyes. He and Lisa were under the covers, snuggled up tight, and dead to the world. Life had exhausted them both, and they were right where they wanted to be.

Bombay was the last in line. He looked up at the missing tile, and then over at Jaime. He followed the rest as they made their way out the front door, but stopped, turned, and walked back into the bedroom. He very gently pulled the covers back, and it was just as he'd thought, the cross was missing from around Jaime's neck.

The boxcars bucked and rocked her against the frame as the train slowly pulled away. She held onto the side and sat with her legs hanging out the door, lit a cigarette, and filed another town and another experience away in her mind. Jaime was alive, and she promised to come back to see him and these mountains in the following spring. She lifted his cross from her neck and began to think, "Maybe there's something to this…" when the sound of a pack landing onto the wooden floor spun her around with a fright. The opposite boxcar door was open, and she saw him running alongside the train. She watched with indifference as he lifted himself up and climbed on board.

"Almost didn't make it!" he said, as he dusted himself off, grabbed his pack, and sat down in the opposite corner from her. "Don't wanna get run over by a train."

"No, I guess not."

"You headin' south?"

"Yeah."

"Me too. Name's Ezra."

"I'm Dito."

"I see you wear a cross. You religious?"

Acknowledgements

This book would not have been possible without the help and influence of others.

I want to thank my dear friend Bethanie Poe for her help in turning what could easily have been another boring autobiography into a readable novel. If it's any good, you can thank her as well. Not only did she help me tell this story in a better way, but she gently pressed me to finish it during the stretches when my motivation was weak at best. As always, she's been a source of encouragement and self-confidence.

To all of you who have knowingly or unknowingly pulled me from the garage over these years. Thank you. Whether it was by casual conversation, reasoning, pleading, or trying to break the door down to get to me, I wouldn't be here now if not for you.

I need to thank the French philosopher, Albert Camus, wherever you may be. Although you've affirmed my suspicions that searching for any meaning to life is absurd, you have nevertheless persuaded me to realize that it can still be worth living. I'm not yet able to imagine Sisyphus happy, but this boulder is all we've got, and just maybe we can each find our own reasons to make it worth pushing up the hill again.

To the homeless and marginalized who welcomed me into your community with love and honesty, I owe to each one of you more than I can put into words. Along with everything this societal structure has stripped from you, with it went your pretensions. You loved me, you made me feel safe, and you made me laugh. You made me feel like I belonged. You shared with me the best that humanity has to offer, and you didn't have to. Thank you.

And to the one who brought me here, the one whom my father would tell me, sometime after her death, that she thought the sun rose and set on me. My mother. I think it's true that you never fully appreciate something or someone until they're gone. Whatever good there may be in me, I owe so much of it to her. She would be pleased to know that the candle she lit is still burning, and very pleased that the scene at the river may have been considered, but never carried out.

And finally, to Mary. Considering the short time that I was given to know you, you impacted my life in ways that I don't know how to adequately describe. Your death was a watershed moment in my life. There's everything before Mary, and then everything after Mary. Just being in your graceful presence was like resting in an English garden, but being called under the bridge that morning was like finding out that the fool who planted it got drunk, dug it up, and set it on fire. What other explanation could there be? But then you were too good for this world anyway. If for no one but you, I hope there's an afterlife, a place of rest and solace, the home you'd hoped for.

Thank you for your patience, for your smiles, and your calming hand as I strung together incoherent rants about the injustices of this world.

Wait for me.

Je suis presque là